MR. DIRTY

NANA MALONE

DEDICATION

To my girl Amy Daws. For these bomb ass covers. But also for being you and always being open to deep shit. Together we make the perfect person. Love you.

BACK COVER

I have a dirty mouth. That's the truth. Women love it. And I have no plans on changing. Why would I?

I like my life. The women, the partying, the fun.

Until I meet my new neighbour.

She's messing with my good thing. She's annoying, and persistent, and a pain in the…well you get the idea. She's also gorgeous, and smart…and completely immune to me.

And now she needs my help with a little Ex payback and I'm more than happy to lend my expertise. Now all I have to do is keep from falling for her in the process. How hard can that be?

1

Nathan knew it was coming.

For over a week, his father had been distracted. Disorganized. Even missed a few meetings. So that meant that any moment now, the old man would come running into his office and beg him to handle whatever it was. Nathan wasn't sure why, but the old man was definitely checking out. Funny thing was, Nathan handled most of the new business that came in. His father was the name, but he was essentially the face. They didn't call him 'The Closer' for nothing.

So, what was the old man working on that had him so distracted? Even his assistant never seemed to know where he was. And the kicker of it was that Nathan was good at what he did. He had a way of getting the clients excited about the partnership. After all, he was a Windsor. The name alone often had people seeing pound symbols. But he had a genuine enthusiasm for some of the projects. But he didn't want to do this for the rest of his life. Windsor Corp. was his father's dream. Not his.

After he closed with the clients, he handed them off to a VP. He wasn't the deep dive person. And if he were honest, anything more than the surface fun stuff of what it could do and what the potential was, bored him silly. Getting into the nitty-gritty of details was not his forte. But he knew when to delegate so things ran smoothly. And at the end of day, the bottom line was all that mattered. So he went on instinct, on what genuinely excited him. The old man didn't even weigh in anymore.

Windsor Corporation had several arms: technology, wellness, beauty—hell, even a liquor division. Luckily for him, it spoke to his strengths. He liked to keep things inter-esting and dynamic. *You get bored.* Yeah, that too. *Because this isn't what you really want to do.* He shut the thought down quickly. Not that he couldn't do what he really wanted to do, but this company—his parents had started it. And with his mother gone, the guilt ate away too much at him. But he couldn't just leave his father.

Even at your own expense? Challenged a part of him. Not at his expense. He had a great life. He loved this company. More often than not whenever he looked at a new product he wanted to feel it was something his mother would have been excited about. Even after all these years it hurt to think about her.

Sure enough, the summons happened just as Nathan was about to head out to meet his mate and accountant Garrett. "You pinged me, Dad?"

His father ran a hand through his hair. "Yeah, listen, I

know it's the height of holiday party season, and I hate to ask again but—"

"Let me guess: you need me to take care of the Milton Meeting?"

His father nodded absently as he ran a hand through his hair and stared grumpily at his laptop. "I'm sorry but something has come up. Do you mind?" Unfortunately, Nathan recognized the pattern. He'd seen it before. After Nathan's mother had died, his father promised him that he was going to change. But something was off.

"You all right there, Dad?"

"Yeah, I'm just looking at the projections for next year. Trying to wrap my head around it."

Nathan narrowed his gaze. "Is there anything you want me to run you through? I can have James up here."

His father shook his head. "No, no. You go ahead. You know, do what you do, woo the client. Bring in the new business. I'll deal with this."

"Are you sure? Because it's not a bother. I can—"

"No, Nathan. I'm fine. Just do your job." And that was the crux of it.

That distance between the two of them. The sting of pain was swift and immediate and sliced right through him. But immediately, he locked it down. He knew just how to assuage that particular brand of pain his father was good at dealing out. "Yep, on it." He left his father in his office and headed straight to the elevator. He just climbed into a company car to take him over to Thrive nightclub. Once he was done with the client, he was going to make sure to dull the pain the only way he knew how. Booze and women. Oh, he'd get the client on board. Get them to sign on the dotted line. Show them a great time. But he was also going to have some fun while doing it.

Settling back in the plush leather seats of the black Mercedes, Nathan closed his eyes and tried to dull the throbbing that was starting to poke him between the eyes. All he had to do was get to the club, and he'd feel better. A little distance between him and the old man was probably a good thing right about now.

He reached for his phone to text his best friend Garrett to meet him at Thrive. But when he patted down his pockets, he found—Shit, he'd had his phone when he went into his father's office, right? He mentally ran through his actions as he tried to get everything straight in his head. He'd been standing in the doorway, walked over to the desk and—Oh bugger.

He leaned forward and tapped his driver Adam on the shoulder. "Yeah, sorry mate. We need to turn back. I left my bloody phone."

Adam nodded. "Not a bother at all. Just a moment." At the next light, he made a right and a U-turn, taking them back in the direction of central London towards the office. Within five minutes, they were out front at the chrome and steel building of Windsor Corporation.

"I'll be right back," Nathan muttered.

He was out of the car in moments and striding through the glass front doors. Security waved him through without even looking up and he was in the elevator in moments. When he reached the thirteenth floor, he hooked to the left toward his father's office, walking briskly. He checked his watch. He'd still have time to make it to the club to meet the client, but he hated to be late. Worse though, he hated feeling like he was missing out on something. The event they were all attending started at ten. It was 9:15 p.m. . He had time, but he didn't like the added time constraints on him.

What the hell was that sound? When he rounded the corner, his stomach dropped. Groaning, moaning and slapping sounds.

No. Please, fucking hell, no. His brain tried to rationalize. *It's not what you think it is. Your ears are playing tricks on you. You are only hearing what you're imagining yourself doing in the next couple of hours.* But the closer he got to his father's office, the more he knew that awful truth.

But he needed the confirmation. Needed to know if his own personal nightmare was coming true. It was like picking at a healing scab. It hurt, and it was gross and disgusting. And bugger, no one ever wanted to see what happened when you peeled off that scab. But it was a compulsion—a desperate need to have a thought confirmed.

The sound only grew in intensity as he neared the corner office, but he still couldn't stop himself. When he reached his father's door, it was closed. Thank fuck. But was Nathan about to get the nightmare scenario of a lifetime?

He only hesitated for a moment before turning the knob. He needed his bloody phone. So, like it or not, he was going in. Besides, the table was right next to the door. He could open the door, grab his phone and be out in seconds. He didn't even have to look. *But you know what's going on, don't you?*

Stop it. Stop it. Stop it. He didn't want to think about it. He didn't want to do that to himself. But it was unavoidable. He couldn't help it. The moment he opened the door, he knew why his father was so out of it. For *months*, he'd *known*. He pretended he didn't know. His brain had offered alternative theories, lies that he could use to soothe the disgust and disdain. Unfortunately, the truth had a way of making it difficult to lie to yourself even with the door open merely a crack. Barely enough for him to squeeze his hand in to grab his phone and turn back around, he saw his father screwing their new head of marketing on top of his desk.

The old man hadn't changed at all, despite all the lies he'd told Nathan. *"This time it will be different." "I've changed."* After years of watching his father hurt his mother — of his father swearing her death had changed him and that he would never cheat again, would never tear apart their family—this was the last straw.

Nathan was forced to swallow the bullshit, and the lies, and the pain. The moment Nathan had his phone in his hand, he and his father locked eyes. The old man's eyes widened, and Nathan's glared. And that was the extent of their exchange.

Once Nathan had his phone, he turned around and marched toward the elevator knowing he could never erase what had just happened.

~

COME ON, *where was he?* Sophie Collins shifted from foot to foot. She'd had to beg to put her boyfriend Christopher on the guest list for this event. Normally, as the events manager, she could invite who she liked. But, as one of the royals was actually going to be here, and it was just before the holidays, tickets for this were like an all access pass to an African diamond mine. She stood on tiptoes in her wedges to see over the crowd, but that was sort of useless as she was only 5'4". But she couldn't find him in the sea of people.

Guests milled about with their flutes of champagne and she did a subconscious check to make sure there were enough appetizers floating around. There was also a sushi bar off to the right. She'd managed to score a chocolate flavored champagne fountain.

Chocolate flavored champagne. Who would have thought? But it was a thing, and it was actually delicious. And every time she looked over there, glasses were going like cupcakes.

She caught the eye of one of the waiters and then inclined her head toward the quickly vanishing glasses and he nodded that he understood he had to go replenish them. Just because she was anxious about her boyfriend showing up didn't mean she still couldn't do her job.

The decorations were festive but understated. Classy. The event was a yearly fundraiser and the client wanted to make it nondenominational. So she opted for lights. Lots of lights. Sting lights, tea lights, muted track lights. And all over there were silent nods to the season.

Sophie had worked for Glass Slipper Events for the last

three years, right out of Uni. And she'd been lucky as all hell to get this gig. She always worked her arse off. She'd gotten the job by working her friendship to Allison, so a part of her always felt like a fraud.

The good news was that Allison and her partner, Deborah loved her. The bad news was she constantly waited for them to find out she had no idea what she was doing.

She'd met Allison in her second year at Uni when she'd snuck into a club. Granted, there had been a guy behind that excursion. One that she'd had a major crush on and who had no idea she existed. Her flatmate at that time had the grand idea that if they just snuck into a club, then she'd sidle up to him, he would notice her and they would have a grand affair. Things hadn't exactly worked out that way.

The bloke, Harrison Weabley, hadn't noticed her. Matter of fact, he'd spilled a Cosmo down her back and hadn't so much as apologized for it. As a result, she'd squealed and bumped into the girl in front of her. That girl was Allison. Of course, being polite, Sophie had apologized. Allison got wind of what happened and actually helped her out. The two of them then formed a friendship. Allison had been just an event coordinator then herself. And they'd kept in touch. The next thing Sophie knew, she had a job out of school. Not bad for a girl from St. Albans.

Growing up she hadn't had very much money. She'd had zero access to places like this. It had all seemed like a dream really. She had gotten a scholarship to Uni, which should have been fantastic. But she hadn't had any money for any extras, so she had to have a job like everyone else.

Trying to make it through because her mother couldn't afford to just give her whatever she wanted.

Now she catered to the stupidly rich. Full circle moment. Money apparently couldn't buy you good looks or taste. No skin off her back really. She would just take the funds and stockpile them away.

She'd always marveled at how Allison always seemed to have a well of cash somewhere. She had her own company. But wouldn't it be smarter to save some of it? It was none of Sophie's business of course. Allison could buy as many Miu-Miu bags as she liked. Sophie, however, would buy a knockoff, or buy a last season one from a charity shop and save her money.

The dream she never told anyone about was running her own events company one day, kind of like what Allison had. But one that had charity in mind. Yes, she was good at her job and she actually did enjoy it. But endlessly supplying chocolate champagne to people was not her end goal. She wanted to do things that helped people too. Like NGOs and providing scholarships.

Yeah, you'll get to that, but first focus on the job at hand, the one in front of you. Stop daydreaming and stop looking for Christopher.

Christopher. Just even thinking about him right now twisted her stomach in knots. He had been her boyfriend for over a year and he was great. Okay, perhaps *great* was the wrong word for it. He was perfectly nice. Solid. Sort of handsome. He occasionally worked out. And by work out she meant he went for a brisk stroll in the English air. But he was perfectly nice. They were well suited. He didn't have any vices, and he had a stable and steady job. He was perfect—just exactly what she needed.

Never mind that he wasn't exciting, or particularly fun, or at times like this made her feel as if he didn't even want to be with her. He knew how important this event was to her. Why the hell would he be late?

You know he's not coming.

No, she didn't *know* he wasn't coming. She had to believe he was coming. She only told him twenty times. Mentioning that a member of royalty was going to be in attendance should have done it. He had been starstruck. Who would give up a chance to be in the same room as royalty? Honestly.

She made another final sweep of the room when she realized he wasn't there. He really *was* standing her up. She always thought she picked well with Christopher. He was the kind of guy who was supposed to be reliable. *Unlike your father.*

She didn't need excitement. She didn't need unpredictability. She had enough of that growing up. But here she was at one of the biggest events of her career, and her boyfriend was a no-show. She stepped out onto the balcony grabbing a flute of champagne on her way. She didn't normally drink at events. But right about now, she needed the fortification. She still had two more hours to go being on duty. It was only eleven o'clock. The party would go on for a while. She'd limit herself to just the one, as always. But hell, she wanted more than just the one.

There were only three other people on the wide stone balcony at that time. Two of them were a couple snogging in one corner. Bloody fantastic. She had no choice really but to stand near the bloke who was leaning on the stone balcony holding a highball glass with some amber liquid.

"Sorry. I don't mean to disturb you. I just needed some air and I have a feeling I'm going to get a show I'm not particularly interested in at the other end."

He lifted his head and glanced down at the other end before chuckling. "Oh, come on. Those two are pretty tame."

Sophie shifted her glance back to the couple. "Are you taking the piss? Any second now, he's about to slip his hand up her skirt."

"Oh, come on, that's not even adventurous. When they start removing items of clothing, that's when I'd worry."

Sophie shuddered. "I have no idea how they can even do that. There are hundreds of people here."

He shrugged. "Sometimes life is fueled by alcohol and bad decisions."

She chuckled. "Down the hatch then." She downed the champagne and immediately wished she hadn't. The bubbles went to her nose and head straight away, causing her to wince.

The dark-haired guy next to her lifted his gaze and turned his attention on her. Sophie could feel the heat of his stare and turned to meet it. *Oh bugger.* Stormy blue eyes bored into her. And for some reason she felt naked and vulnerable. "I see you don't drink often," he muttered.

Sophie frowned. "What?"

He nodded at her glass and a lock of his dark, silky hair fell on his brow. "You should know better than to guzzle down champagne like that. You will end up with a headache."

"Oh yeah, I was just thinking that. And no, I don't drink often. But I needed it tonight."

He nodded and held up his glass. "I understand. Next time try scotch. It will go down smoother. Minus the headache if you just have the one."

"I'll take that under advisement." With eyes full of smoke and steel he pushed himself to standing, and she couldn't help but stumble back a step as he spoke. "I'm Nathan."

Dear Lord. The man was—Jesus Christ people, they made men like this? He looked like something legitimately out of a catalogue. For starters, he was very tall—over six feet at least, lean, soccer player or tennis player kind of build. His thick dark hair curled slightly on the ends. Sculpted cheekbones and strong jaw, combined with deep set eyes framed by dark sooty lashes completed the godlike appearance. *And* he was talking to her. Shit, he'd asked her a question. Bugger, what was it?

His full lips tipped into a lopsided smirk. "Who is it you're waiting for?"

Sophie frowned. "Excuse me?"

The smile only deepened as he crossed his arms and leaned against the railing. "My guess is a boyfriend. He's late, is he?"

Sophie shook her head. "I'm sorry, I don't even—"

But Nathan wasn't listening. "I mean, if you were my girl ... " His gaze slid over her body, and it felt like lightning caressed her synapses. " ... I would be early, every single time." He leaned forward and lowered his voice so only she could hear him. "Except in bed, of course. There, I'd take my time. Make sure you got there first, twice, probably three times. I'd like you to enjoy yourself."

Panties down. Panties down! Sophie couldn't move. She knew she *should* move. Knew that what he was saying to her was dirty. And, well, hot. And oh, so inappropriate. But still, she didn't move. She couldn't move. Her feet were rooted, bolted to the cement beneath her. "I—I don't know what you—"

"You don't know what I mean? I'm talking about in bed. You're busy staring at the door; I already saw you earlier, busy looking for someone to show up. And honestly, he's an idiot if he has left you here on your own. Someone like me might come up and sweep you into my bed."

She blinked, hoping that the small action would give her brain a second to catch up. He was flirting. Well, forget flirting; he was downright forward. And inappropriate and there was a part of her that liked it, even though she shouldn't. "You can't say that to me." Why was her voice husky and whisper hot?

He shrugged. "Why not?"

"You don't even know me. And it's a bit rude."

He grinned and Sophie swore to God she almost dropped her knickers. "It's not rude if you like it. And given by the flush in your cheeks, and the way your pupils have dilated, I think you do like it. Does Mr. Late and Stupid talk to you like this?"

No, Christopher never spoke to her like this. But that

was beside the point. "Is my boyfriend rude and forward? No, he's not."

"No, he's just late.

"To me, that classifies as rude. He's also clearly stupid, if he would leave someone like you waiting." He leaned closer. "What do you say? Why don't you chuck him over? I'm here. I can be your boyfriend for the night."

For the night. Her boyfriend.

It wasn't her fault. It was her brain. Traitorous eyes offered images of Nathan doing dirty things to her with his mouth and his hands. Those long, sculpted fingers looked sure. As if they were practiced, skilled. It wasn't cheating if she thought about it. That was just imagination. She would never chuck Christopher for some fit as hell bloke who said dirty things to her on a balcony. After all, how many dirty things had he said to other women tonight? Besides, she knew the type all too well. That was a good point.

"So, is your dirty talk reserved just for me, or is it just because I'm handy?" She cocked her head.

His chuckle was low and throaty and made her nipples contract. Oh hell, he couldn't see her nipples through her dress, could he? She was wearing a strapless dress with a bra, but the bra had barely any padding in it.

"All that matters is I'm talking to you now." And then his gaze slid off her body. They hovered for just a second over her breast, and hell. He could her tightened nipples. When he lifted his gaze to her eyes again, he winked. "It seems you like the way I'm talking to you."

"I'm going to go back inside now." *Way to be firm, Sophie.*

He cocked his head. "You're sure about that?"

Nope. "Yes, yes. Very, very, sure."

Nathan shrugged. "Too bad. It would have been fun." He downed his drink and then studied her. "Just so you know, you deserve better than some git who doesn't pay attention to you and doesn't give you what you need. Not that what I'm telling you will matter."

What the hell? "You don't know anything about me."

"You're wrong about that. I know you're wasting your time on a guy who doesn't deserve you."

Sophie frowned and turned her back to him. Whatever. That guy didn't know her at all.

2

———

Nathan had struck out.

He wasn't used to that. It didn't matter, though. Not like there weren't plenty of women here. *Oh yeah? Then why do you keep looking at the redhead with the big green eyes?* He wasn't. He told himself he wasn't. His dick, on the other hand, begged to differ. *Fine whatever.* The client meeting had gone well. They had some brand-new technology app. Even better security for your home. He told them to submit an RFP because at the end of the day, Windsor already had a similar product, though this one promised to be at a cheaper price point. So, it was worth further investigation. So now, he was basically here to play, or lose himself for an hour.

He didn't have to wait long. The bartender who had given him the whiskey earlier caught his eye again and gave him a wide smile. When he strolled up to her, he leaned over. "Are you going to pour me another drink?"

She grinned. "Are you going to give me another hundred quid tip?"

He grinned. "Depends on how well you pour." She leaned forward, crossing her arms, making sure to squeeze her tits together and giving him a fantastic view down her low slung pink top.

"You do realize the drinks are free, right?"

He widened his eyes and let his mouth hang open. "Are you sure? I had no idea. Can I have my tip back?"

She laughed low. "You absolutely can, if you can find it."

"Oh, I promise. I'm very good at finding things. It'll only take me seconds."

She lifted her brow. "Seconds, is it? You're so sure of yourself."

Nathan knew they weren't talking about the tip he'd left her. If they ever had been. She was challenging him. "I promise you less than ten."

"Well, I'm going on a break in a minute. You want to show me your fantastic skills?"

"Abso-fucking-lutely!" Except he didn't really want to. It was more like scratching a mild itch. She would do. She was pretty. *She's not the redhead.* Damn it. He didn't want to think about her.

Once the bartender found him ten minutes later, she tugged him down the hall toward the coat check. As it was the middle of August and unseasonably warm outside, no one had any coats to check. "It looks like you're leading me in here for nefarious reasons," he teased.

"You have ten minutes to wow me or forever tarnish your reputation." Nathan wasted no time. He backed her up against one of the counters, lifted her onto it and had his hands smoothing up her thighs. If he closed his eyes, he could pretend she was someone else. The woman he actually wanted.

She smelled wrong, though. Her perfume was too thick. Too flowery, but he didn't care. When his thumbs found the edges of her knickers, he smirked as her eyes widened. "What, you really don't think I can do it?"

Her grin was easy. "Let's just say I think you have your work cut out for you." She tipped her head up for a kiss.

"Oh, ye of little faith." Nathan knew what he was doing. He leaned forward even as his thumbs teased the edges of her panties. Instead of kissing her, he nuzzled that spot just below her ear and then nipped her earlobe lightly. "Get ready to scream."

All it took was a simple teasing brush over her clit and a bite at her earlobe as he slid one finger inside her. When he applied pressure to both her clit and the bundle of nerves inside, he bit her ear again, and she screamed. Instead of the husky voice of the redhead on the balcony, her voice was higher pitched, more of a squeal. He forced himself to focus.

You have a woman who is about to be sitting on your dick, coming around your fingers. Focus. He dragged his attention to the task at hand. He could feel her inner walls clamping around his finger and then he added another.

Her fingertips dug into his shoulders as her hips rode his fingers. "Yes! Oh my God! Oh my God! Oh my God!"

"That's five seconds. You want another one?"

She didn't answer him verbally. Just clamped her legs

tighter around his fingers and then widened them deliberately as she nodded.

"Yeah, I thought you might." He dragged out his wallet, pulled out a condom quickly, dispensed with the foil in seconds, and had himself shielded. "Is this what you want?"

She nodded furiously.

"Oh no you don't. Say the words. Say 'I want you to fuck me.'"

"Jesus. I want you to fuck me. Just hurry up." He chuckled to himself as he eased his fingers out of her. She moaned low. Then he stepped between her legs, dug his hands into her hair and then sank in deep. He closed his eyes, trying to focus just on the sensation. She was soft, needy, and enthusiastic. A little too enthusiastic maybe. There was a part of him that wanted to work for it a little. Like with that redhead. She'd probably have *him* begging. He wasn't sure what it was, but something made him open his eyes.

Oh hell, it was her. The redhead. Through what was supposed to be the open window of the coat check, he could see her in the doorway, and she was watching him. Their eyes locked. From where he stood, he couldn't see her pupils, but he knew they were dilated. Her lips were parted, and he watched the rise and fall of her chest as her breathing grew more and more ragged.

As he fucked the nameless blonde, he watched her, the one he wanted. She watched him. And he couldn't help but imagine that *she* was the one he was touching. That she had taken him up on his offer. That she had chosen *him* over the guy who stood her up. That she was the one in here with him, her center, clamped around his dick and moaning in his ear.

He should have stopped. She should have turned away. But neither of them seemed to be able to stop what they were doing. And he couldn't help finding perverse pleasure in her watching him.

He wanted to know things about her. He wanted to know how she liked it. Did she like it dirty? Even as he deepened his strokes, he leaned closer to the blonde and said loudly enough for the other woman to hear, "Do you like it dirty? Do you like when I talk to you?" The blonde moaned something unintelligible in his ear. The redhead bit her lip.

Oh yeah, she liked it dirty.

He reached his hand around to tap the blonde's arse, bringing them closer together. Jesus, she had a vice grip on him. And while it felt good, she wasn't exactly what he wanted. He was irritated enough about that to nip her shoulder, making her gasp. As for Red, she looked like she was squeezing her thighs together.

Hell yes. When his fingertips *accidentally/not so* accidentally grazed the pucker of the blonde's arse. She gave a low, hissing moan. But he was studying the redhead. Her lips parted again, and her tongue flipped out to lick her bottom lip. *Shit.* Would she want him to do this? Would she let him? Just the thought of it had the electricity crackling up his spine. Fuck.

He might be a twat, fucking one girl while eye fucking another, but he had a reputation to uphold. And so, the girl he was actually fucking needed to come before he could, and he was too damn close. Reaching his other hand between them, he flipped his thumb quickly over her clit and clenched his teeth, holding off the orgasm until he could feel her clamping around him again. Little quivers squeezing him again, and again, and again. He lifted his gaze back to the redhead and came on a low, harsh growl.

Jesus Christ, he was going to die. An orgasm was actually going to kill him. But he knew it wasn't because of the girl he was with. It was because of the girl with the big green eyes. When his brain finally started to come back online, he lifted his eyes to see if she was still watching him, but she was gone. The disappointment hit him swiftly. He'd wanted her to stay, but she was gone— as if she'd never been there to begin with.

3

One Year Later ...

Sophie tossed in bed.

It was hot and stifling in her flat. But she wasn't going to open the window as the noise from outside would be far worse than the heat. This was London. No one had air conditioning. But it wasn't the heat getting to her.

She knew what her problem was. She was frustrated. Sexually frustrated. She and Christopher had been off again. They haven't had sex in nearly two months. Not that anything was wrong per se; it was just that their schedules were a mess. They weren't meshing well. When he did stay over, he never seemed particularly interested in sex. Not that she was either. They just had to connect.

That's not the real reason.

Damn it. She didn't want to think about why.

Okay, fine. That wasn't the real reason. The real reason was Nathan flipping Windsor. She might have been mildly obsessed with her neighbor across the hall. Everything about this flat was perfect, exactly what she wanted. Everything except him. After that fateful meeting at Thrive a year ago, things had been off-kilter. But then he'd moved in six months ago. He was a pain in the arse. He was loud. He was fresh. And he didn't remember her at all. That stung the worst.

The day he'd moved in, she'd gone over to be neighborly. And then she'd come face-to-face with the man she'd watched shagging someone else while he eye-fucked her. Not that he belonged to her or anything. Hell, she *had* a boyfriend. But that night played in her head over and over again. It was her go-to thought or memory when she was sexually frustrated. Between that and her vibrator, getting a little relief from the sexual tension was easy.

You watched him shag someone. Just the idea of it made her flush.

He'd been so locked on her, as if he'd been thinking about her the entire time, which she knew was rubbish. He hadn't, of course. He was just that kind of guy who would do anything, screw anyone, in the moment.

But when she'd gone over to say, "Hey neighbor," she'd been shocked to find him on the other side, looking completely unfazed. And then come to find out he was the neighbor from hell.

The problem was, she could hear *everything* that happened in his flat. The walls in this building were paper-thin. This building with a highly coveted unit in Soho and built over a club. While the floors were soundproofed, the walls were not. So, while she didn't hear that many comings and goings from downstairs, she could practically hear everything that he did.

The units in this floor where L-shaped so they shared a bedroom wall and then a common corridor, a sort of a waiting area. And then there were the stairs that went down. They also had a shared space rooftop garden up above. Something she rarely ever took advantage of.

She always imagined she'd find him up there shagging his latest conquest and busy not remembering her. Not that she cared. She could hear everything that was happening in his bedroom anyway.

Sophie had even tried putting on headphones. Those stupid things were supposed to be noise canceling. But it didn't matter what she played. She could still *imagine* what he was doing. It had been driving her slowly insane for months. She could imagine the moans, imagine that look in his eye as he screwed that other woman, where his fingers had gone, how he'd seem to dare her, to question her. Asking if she liked to be touched ... there. If she would let him touch her. If she would let him tease her like that. *Oh God!*

Why couldn't she get him out of her head? She didn't even like him.

4

The jarring thud of repetitive bass first filtered into Sophie's dream. It thrummed so loud she could feel it into her bones. She was at a club and it was crowed, hot and noisy. *Too* crowded hot and noisy.

She was looking for someone through the white cloud of a choking smoke machine, pointlessly trying to call their name over the deafening music. Gradually, elements of her dream began to fade away and she became aware that she was lying in her bed.

Slowly, like emerging from underwater, the people, the darkness and the smoke began to shimmer and disappear. Gradually, everything was gone. Except for the music. Her bed almost vibrated with the bass. *Hang on.*

Sophie snapped open her eyes.

She most definitely *wasn't* in a club. She was most definitely in the warm cocoon of her bed and it was … She reached for her phone to check … 2:15 a.m. So why the hell could she still hear music? *You know why.*

"Jesus Christ," she muttered. Unfortunately, she knew why she could still hear music. And she knew exactly where it was coming from.

Swinging her legs around, she yanked her dressing gown from the bedpost and threw it on, fury building in her veins.

"I'm going to kill him," she muttered, marching across her room, down the hallway and out of her front door.

Directly opposite her was the closed door of her neighbor's flat. The music was much louder here. Threads of guitar mingled with the bass, cementing the scowl on Sophie's face. Closing her hand into a fist, she pounded at the door.

What the hell was wrong with him? Seriously. He had to be doing this on purpose. She wished she could say this was the first time she'd had to run over here in the middle of the night.

The guy was inconsiderate. *Sexy.* An arsehole. *Hotter than Satan.* Arrogant. And Sexy … *You already said sexy.* Shit. It didn't matter. Sexy or not, with abs that could shred her clothes, he was a full-on wanker.

It stayed shut. She pounded again, for longer this time. "For God's sake, Nathan, answer the door," she yelled. Just as she'd lifted her arm to hammer at it again, it swung open, revealing a man, completely starkers.

"Hey neighbor." Nathan grinned.

She'd seen him shirtless before. Hell, he practically ran around that way all the damn time. He worked out shirtless. He lounged by the pool upstairs shirtless. He barbecued … shirtless. But this was the first time she had seen

Nathan completely naked and, she had to be honest, it threw her.

Happy Christmas to me. Dear lord, half naked didn't even do justice to the man. For the sake of Christ, he was fucking outstanding. She thought back to the scene in that movie *Crazy, Stupid, Love* when Emma Stone saw Ryan Gosling's body, gasped, and then asked him if he was photoshopped.

Well, you can take Ryan Gosling's body and double it. No, quadruple it, she thought, scanning Nathan as best she could using her peripheral vision only.

God damn it. He is well fit. She swore she didn't mean to. But her eyes betrayed her and inadvertently shifted to his man parts. Her mouth fell open again. Seriously, that thing had to be some kind of joke. It was massive. No way in hell any woman could take that. And hell, it seemed *huge.* And it was pointing right at her.

Sophie suddenly realized that her arm was still suspended in midair, forgotten about as she carried out her not-so-subtle perv. Lowering it down to her side, she resolutely forced her gaze onto his eyes.

I will not give him the satisfaction of seeing me check out his body. Or his penis ... Oh my God, his penis. I mean the thing was ... No. What an arrogant prick, answering the door with nothing on. I mean, what an inflated bloody ego.

She cleared her throat, trying to stop the barrage of thoughts in her head and focus. "Nathan," she said coolly, her tone dangerous, "this is the third fucking time you've woken me up in the middle of the night this week. Have some bloody respect and keep your music down. Some of us have work in the morning. *Some* of us have jobs to go to."

Nathan held his hands up in surrender.

Don't look down, Sophie repeated over and over to herself. *Just look at his face.*

"And there was me thinking you were coming over to join the party?" Nathan drawled, his smooth accent speaking of years of the best British boarding schools and access to all that privilege could buy.

She gawped at him. "I don't think so. Can you just keep the noise down? Please? I am begging you. I'm so damn tired that I will give you anything to turn it down. I mean—"

Before she'd even finished speaking, a tall, porcelain-skinned brunette wearing a thong and a smile snaked up to him and started running her hands over his pectoral muscles, blatantly and rudely ignoring Sophie.

Nathan laughed. "I'm not sure I can make any promises about keeping the noise down." He smiled slowly, his steely blue eyes meeting Sophie's with an unwavering confidence. "But I will reduce the volume of the music." He backed away and shut the door, leaving Sophie standing there, stunned.

Shaking her head in bewilderment, she stalked back over the communal hallway and into her own flat, having to fight the urge to childishly slam her door behind her.

The absolute nerve of the guy. She flicked her kettle on for tea, now that she was far too wound up to sleep. *Who on earth answers the door with no clothes on? The arrogance, the sheer … barefaced cheek.* She allowed herself a little chuckle at her joke, plopping a teabag into the cup.

She would be a wreck for work tomorrow. Luckily, she didn't have an event but still. Sophie had been beside herself with joy when her company had offered her this flat at cut-rate rent. She'd have to sell several kidneys on the black market to afford to pay for the place at full price, but work had wanted her close by and amongst the action, so they'd let it to her cheap as part of her contract.

Being an events manager for Glass Slipper Events meant that she had to have her finger on the pulse when it came to trends in nightlife. Part of her job was to go out drinking with friends and discover where was popular and what music was playing. Her boss needed her to be on trend to help impress clients. Her job was awesome. At least, that's what her friends and family kept telling her, and what she had to keep remembering to tell herself.

Yes, she enjoyed it. There was something hugely satisfying about organizing and arranging an event that blew everybody's mind, but Sophie didn't find it particularly fulfilling.

If she were honest, sometimes the shallowness of it all got her down. The clients were *stupid rich* and *stupid, stupid*. They cared more about the brand of champagne at a party than they did their own families sometimes. Sophie found that, as a whole, they were a despairing breed of the human race. Self-important and self-entitled.

Still, she was damn good at what she did, and because of it she had bagged herself a massive flat bang smack in the middle of Soho.

Her place was above a huge, pretentious underground bar. The company certainly wasn't lying when they said they wanted her close to the action. There was only one other flat besides hers, the one opposite, the one she currently wished was still empty.

She still couldn't believe her luck that the guy she'd watched was her neighbor. Worse, he didn't remember her at all. Not that she'd expect him too. Likely, he did shit like that all the time.

He was breathtakingly striking. Handsome was putting it too mildly. Even gorgeous felt like an understatement when she was trying to describe him to her best friend the day after she'd first seen him.

"He's seriously fit. To the point where if I have to talk to him I might not be able to stop myself from touching his face."

Her friend Gemma had squealed down the phone. "That's it. I'm coming over."

"Hey, I saw him first. Besides, he's an arrogant git," Sophie protested.

"Uh, you have a boyfriend, you slag. I'm the single, sad and lonely one. The least you could do is let me hang around outside your flat for a couple of days, so I can check him out."

Sophie had laughed and promised Gemma she'd introduce her to him. Not that she intended to intentionally speak to him. She was more apt to kill him first.

~

AFTER BRIANNA PASSED out from orgasm number he'd-lost-count, Nathan lay in bed scowling. He should be asleep. Contrary to what his uptight neighbor thought, he had a big day tomorrow too. He just had a later start.

And how the hell was he supposed to know she was home? Nine times out of ten she got home later than he did. And that was saying something.

Hell, he should be thinking about the woman in his bed. The girl was a bloody supermodel. But no, his mind was on his uptight as fuck neighbor from across the hall. He'd felt her gaze on him. It was hot and familiar and made him want to tug her blond locks. That gaze reminded him of the sexy redhead from that night.

Fuck. Instant hard-on.

It was next to impossible not to replace Brianna's image with hers as he'd fucked the model into a stupor. Didn't matter what he tried. He couldn't shake the sense of familiarity with neighbor Sophie.

He scrubbed his hands over his face. He needed to get it together. His brain took him to that first day he met her.

As he'd crossed her on the stairs, he couldn't help but look his female neighbor up and down out of habit. *Tight body, even if it's been hidden underneath that God-awful coat,* he'd thought. So much of fashion was bullshit. He preferred women in their natural state: naked.

He'd clocked the curves beneath the thick material. Her blond hair had been pulled off her face in a chunky bun. But it was her almond-shaped green eyes that had stopped him cold. There'd been a hint of recognition in them. And he was dying to know more.

She'd bumped right into him. Or he, into her. He hadn't been able to explain the feeling, but he'd wanted to keep her in his arms for a moment longer. Given his history, that was one hell of an anomaly.

He'd flashed her his most winning smile. The smile he knew generally worked on women. Then he'd dropped his opening line.

"Hi, gorgeous."

She'd blinked. Then scowled. Then crossed her arms as if waiting for him to come up with something better. Eventually, she'd brushed past him on the way to her flat. "My name is Sophie by the way."

"I'm Nathan."

"Oh, I know."

It wasn't so much that she knew who he was. It was that she seemed to *know* him. And somehow, he'd ticked her off. But how, though? He knew for a fact he hadn't slept with her. He remembered them all.

So, what the hell had he done to her to make her hate him so much?

Over the last nine months, Nathan had tried to reestablish himself on his own. And okay, maybe his bed rarely went empty. But he'd been through every rational reason in the book. There was no reason for her to have such a strong reaction to him.

He'd tried to start conversations and spark up some kind of rapport, but she was completely oblivious to every charm trick he pulled out of his sleeve.

That shit was bloody frustrating. She was completely immune. Maybe that's what he had been waiting for.

Someone to see through his brand of bullshit. Someone to actually see hm. Too bad she found him lacking.

No amount of attempted conversations put her at ease. The girl simply wouldn't thaw out around him. In fact, if at all possible, her layer of ice just grew thicker.

He'd actually started to enjoy sparring with her. He liked getting a rise out of her. Just like she got a rise out of him. Pun intended. He hadn't missed her blatant appraisal of him.

One night, she'd started by banging the shit out of his door because she reckoned his music was too loud. He'd tried to invite her in. His friends had come from Warwickshire and he genuinely wanted her to come and get to know him over a drink.

That was when he'd learned that she was seriously uptight.

Her boyfriend looked like a wound up old fart too, but Nathan was more than familiar with getting the cold shoulder from pretty girls' boyfriends, so he wasn't too fussed. He couldn't say he liked the lad, though. He pretty much had twat written all over him. The two of them barely seemed to spend any time together, anyway. In Nathan's opinion, she could do better.

Sophie had said that she had work in the morning. Who in their right mind had a job where they had to work early on a Saturday? He worked hard, but hell, he knew how to have a good time.

Sophie never had any fun. Ever. He didn't think that he'd ever seen her smile or wear her hair even slightly out of place. Quite literally, he'd never seen her let her hair down. Frankly, he wanted to muss her up in more ways than one.

The only communication between them was a set of terse conversations about him keeping her up all night. *And not in the usual way I'd keep women up too late either.*

Now, the only time Sophie spoke to him was to moan at him for his music being too loud, or because one of his guests was laughing too loudly in the hallway. *I mean, come on. Who on earth gets angry because they hear laughter?* The girl was, quite simply, a pain in his arse. And he wanted to get under her skin. Good thing he had an idea or two how to do that.

5

As Sophie left her flat that morning, as immature as it may have been, she couldn't resist closing her door *hard*. Make that slamming her door especially hard. She gave a snort of laughter, imagining Nathan and his supermodel clutching their sore heads. The way her petty was set up, she went for little digs. It was a satisfying start to her day.

"Stupid, inconsiderate wanker," she muttered as she stepped down each step and out into the day.

The most annoying thing about Nathan was that his late-night, playboy revelries stuck in her head during her entire journey to work and sometimes beyond. Swaying as the tube made its way to Islington and the offices of Glass Slipper Events, the chug of the underground train lulled her deeper into her preoccupied mind.

Seriously, that guy had a different girl at his place almost every single night. How could one man go through so many girls? Never the same one twice, either. He was the sort of guy that Sophie had avoided her whole life. Just like her father.

Every one of his women looked like a model too. And Sophie had met her fair share of models at work. In fact, she even thought she recognized a few. She'd seen them leaving his flat in the morning for their walk of shame. A more elegant, more poised walk of shame than Sophie or her girl-friends had ever done, sure, but a walk of shame none-theless.

A few times, Sophie had been tempted to warn the poor, hyper-skinny souls about what they were letting them-selves in for. Several times, the words 'He's just gonna use you. You're one of hundreds,' formed on her lips, but she never spoke them aloud. *Let them make their own mistakes.*

The vibrating of her phone in her pocket brought her back to attention. It was from Chris, checking that they were still on for that evening. She quickly typed her reply.

Sophie: *Yes, but can we just hang out at mine? Dickhead across the hall woke me up again so I just want a really chill night.*

He replied instantly.

Chris: *Okay.*

She smiled at his perfunctory response. She knew he wasn't being cold. He was just being *Christopher.*

The tube ride was short, and she emerged from the underground blinking wildly as her eyes adjusted to the white light of the autumn morning.

As usual, the office was already buzzing as she stepped into its warmth. Saturdays were prime work days in publicity and events. Most people ended up taking Sundays and Mondays off. People were dashing everywhere, stabbing at iPads without looking up. Sophie trudged blearily to her desk and plonked her handbag onto the table. She'd barely undone three of her coat buttons before her boss came dashing up to her.

"Sophie. I've sent you an email with the details, but I need you to manage an event coming up. It's soon."

Sophie took one look at the desperation in Allison's eyes and sighed.

"How soon?" she asked, although she knew exactly what was coming.

"Two weeks … Uh, New Year's Eve." Allison grimaced, aware that she was giving her a tough assignment. "I know, I know. But the client is really clear on what they want and it's such a big contract for us, with the chance of—"

"Long term work," Sophie finished Allison's sentence, having been on the receiving end of these impossible time frames before.

"Well yes. Quite. Plus, it'll be a breeze for you. Location is already booked and set. It's right underneath your building. The new Bar there. How perfect will that be? No travel time. Their previous Events company booked it, but then couldn't handle the load of the party, so they called us in."

New Year's flipping Eve? Sophie gritted her teeth and forced the corners of her lips up, hoping that resembled a smile. She liked Allison, really. She was a frenetic, highly-strung woman, but as bosses went, she was pretty fair and Sophie knew that she was one of her favorites. After all, they'd sort of come up together. Most of the time Allison felt more like a friend than a boss.

"Brilliant. I get to take my work home with me literally, huh? Okay. I'll do it. You know I'll do it. There just better be no bloody ice sculptures on the list this time."

Allison looked visibly relieved at Sophie's acceptance and then laughed lightly at the memory of Sophie's disaster with the ice sculpture on her last event. They'd been delivered a very pornographic, naked man for a Roman-themed charity dinner.

Sophie had ended up having to shave down the giant ice penis, so it looked a little less like a model for a joke sex toy.

"No ice sculptures, I promise. This one's a breeze in comparison to that."

Finally removing her coat at last, Sophie read through her email to get the specs for the event. Two weeks was a push and would be stressful for her, but New Year's Eve would be next to impossible.

No, not impossible. You can do anything.

It seemed to be a straightforward event, drinks and canapés for a fairly successful internet start-up looking for further investments. Waiters and waitresses would be straightforward, and she had a list of hundreds of award-winning caterers who could take care of food.

The theme was a bit vague. The client had simply listed 'festive jungle,' which made Sophie tut, but at least she could keep it quite simple and build on it if they weren't happy.

She was, though, excited about the venue. Despite living over the top of it, Sophie had never been to the underground bar beneath her. It was one of those bars that was so exclusive, it didn't even have a sign on the outside.

To the uninformed, it just looked like a grand, Edwardian London house in the middle of Soho. To those in the know, it was somewhere that was so cool that it didn't even exist to outsiders. She was curious as to what the inside of a hidden bar might look like, even if she was certain that she would hate the type of hipster that would usually hang out there.

She had already begun to email her wait staff agency while she checked over the rest of the document. And then she froze.

There, on the required invite list from her client, was a name that she had not expected to see.

Nathan Windsor.

"You've got to be fucking kidding me," she whispered at her computer, the email abandoned. Of all the people that she did not want to have to be enclosed in a basement bar with. It had nothing to do with his late-night antics and everything to do with the last event he'd been at. How did he even get invited? It's not like he was one of those Windsors. She frowned, contemplating. No. Couldn't be. This guy was a total lay about. Not some mogul.

Sophie had to check something in a panic. "God damn it."

She pushed her chair back from her desk, ignoring the frowns of her colleagues. The client, the owner of the fancy schmancy, new, hot as shit app that everybody was going to want a piece of was a woman. There would be no convincing her that Nathan was a dick.

He was far, far too good-looking—it was blinding to everybody, including her sometimes. But why in the hell was he on this list of potential investors in this business? It suddenly dawned on Sophie that she knew absolutely nothing about her neighbor other than the fact he was into rock music and brunettes. *And blondes. And redheads.*

~

NATHAN ALMOST FLUNG his phone across the room after yet another argument with his father. It had gone much the same way it always had.

Dad: "Come back to Windsor Corp. I need you. I'll expect you for Christmas Eve Roast and we can discuss it."

Him: "I'm on my own. Get used to it. And I won't be home."

Dad: "You're being immature. We can work out these differences. After all, what the hell are you going to do with yourself?"

As if I hadn't been the one to build Windsor Corp. in the last five years and drag them into modern times. I'd been more than wise with my investments, so my Windsor inheritance could go away tomorrow and I'd still make the Forbes list.

But then, Dad had pulled a fucking low blow bringing up his stepmother.

Dad: You're breaking Judith's heart with what you're doing.

With what he was doing? Nathan shook his head. What a load of bullshit. A friend had said that his father had made the marketing girl a junior associate. He was such a fucking git. And now because of his old man, he had to avoid Judith. He couldn't look her in the eye.

Hell, what he needed tonight was to crash out. He was in desperate need of some distraction and some light-hearted fun after that phone call. As a kid, he'd adored the old man. Wanted to be just like him. Nathan had always admired his father's resilience and perseverance, had always thought that hard work and determination was all you needed to make your family secure and happy. That gold plating had worn after his mother's death.

And now his father was up to his old bullshit all over again. He was going to lose his family over this shit.

Nathan cursed. It wasn't like he had daddy issues or anything weird. He was just disappointed that he'd been let down so spectacularly from the man he'd used to look up to.

But sitting in a funk was not his style. Instead, he got up and headed to his wardrobe. It was time to pick himself back up and move on. He'd deal with the family bullshit later. He sure as hell wasn't going to let it ruin his night. He needed to numb the well of emotion.

Decision made, he reached for his designer jeans and a T-shirt made of a silk blend. It felt smooth against his bare chest. It made him feel good. Not as good as a woman's touch, though.

Striding over to the full-length mirror in his dressing room, he ran his fingers through his dark hair. Yeah, he'd pull tonight. It wouldn't take long. And he'd be able to block all this shit out. Forget about the betrayal.

He scrolled through his address book until he found

what he was looking for. *Canada*. That wasn't her real name of course. He just called her that because that was where he'd met her.

She was a model he had met a couple of weeks back. The next Brazilian *It* girl. But there were so many Brazilian supermodels now. It was hard to keep track.

So, he called her Canada. It was as easy as that. When he needed a date for the evening, someone to let off steam, all Nathan had to do was scroll through his phone and make a call.

Thing was, it wasn't as cold as it seemed. These girls in his phone, they had thrown themselves at him and he was simply obliging. It wasn't always about looks. For him, it was about escapism. Fun. Some laughs. He was always very clear that he would only be around for one night, explained there would be nothing more to it right from the very start. He wasn't mean or cruel. He enjoyed the plea-sure of being with a beautiful woman; he enjoyed fucking and drinking. That didn't make him a bad person. Just a normal bloke in a slightly more advantageous position than most. *It makes you like him*. No. Nathan wasn't hurting anyone.

In all his years, not one woman had drunkenly called or texted him, begging for a second chance. Nathan was proud of that. Twenty-six years old and he'd never been the reason for a woman's tears. He certainly wasn't starting now.

6

Canada was proving to be an extremely good distraction. She was tall and exotically beautiful, and Nathan found her unbelievably sexy. They went for dinner, though, and as was standard, she barely ate anything.

Still, Nathan tucked into his steak while she picked around a salad. He was used to the models he dated nibbling on two pieces of cucumber. But she was nice and chatty and made him laugh a few times. Fortunately, Canada only worked in London a couple of times a year, so she was looking for something as free and easy as he was. It was proving to be the most perfect distraction from the whirl of emotions he was running from.

By the time they'd had several early cocktails, Nathan was feeling a familiar pull. When Canada uncrossed and crossed her legs, revealing an extra couple of inches of her caramel colored thighs, he leaned over. "Why don't you come back to mine and say goodbye to London in style?"

He whispered the proposition into her ear and her skin

broke out in goosebumps. It gave him a shiver of power, of anticipation, knowing that he had that effect on someone. Just like always.

Once they reached his flat, she stared. "Wow," she gasped. "The rent on this must be wicked. What is it you do again?" She turned to him, her brown eyes curious. Truth was, he'd never told her what he did because she hadn't actually asked.

He grabbed a bottle of champagne from his fridge, tipped some ice cubes into a bucket and placed that and two champagne flutes onto a tray.

"I've just started my own business. It's like a consultancy for businesses that need to improve productivity."

His Brazilian beauty frowned momentarily and then laughed. "I just assumed you were a model, like me." She gestured to him. "I mean, look at you. You *should* be a model. You'd put every other male in the industry out of a job."

Nathan smiled, used to hearing these kinds of compliments but enjoying them all the same. "Thanks." He wanted to change the subject from his work.

"Come on. I want to show you the rooftop garden," Nathan said, picking up the tray.

"But it's freezing outside!" Canada looked alarmed.

"Trust me." Nathan grinned. The earlier rain had made the August night cooler than usual.

He loved the rooftop garden. He shared it with Little Miss Uptight. Just like they shared the pool and the hot tub. But he wasn't here for that tonight.

The view from the roof was breathtaking, even for

Nathan, who had seen it a hundred times before. They were fortunate that although the air was cold, the skies were crisp and clear. Before them, the still, cold night revealed a view right across the illuminated skyline of the city.

"This is stunning," Canada breathed.

"I know, right?" Nathan busied himself preparing the area. He'd spent a lot of thought, and money, designing his part of the rooftop garden. There had already been a chair and a little side table up here, presumably belonging to stuck up Sophie, but he had added several, heavy-duty gas flamed outdoor heaters, a chaise lounge, a large coffee table and strings of outdoor lighting. If you're gonna do something, do it well, Nathan had figured. So now the whole area was akin to a climactic scene in a romance movie.

On the inside of the door, there was a large ottoman from which he pulled out several giant sized, faux fur throws and some downy cushions which he threw onto the chaise lounge—making it look invitingly cozy. The flames from the heaters warmed the little section around the seat and gave the whole area an orange, warm glow.

Canada made a happy spin before joining Nathan on the chair and accepting her glass of bubbles with a coy smile. He loved the fact that he could make even the most attractive and confident of girls feel giddy. He liked making someone feel special.

This was his kingdom, his domain. It was what he excelled at. It was all in the details, all about setting the scene.

Briefly, he wondered if he was ever going to meet someone that would make him feel compelled to see them for a second time—or even a third or a forth. He sincerely hoped not. He did not want to run the risk … Nathan turned his attention back to his guest. Now was not the time to be pondering the future; now was the time to be very much in the present.

He took Canada's glass and set it down before leaning in to kiss her.

~

IN A WORD, hectic. That's how her day had gone. With two weeks to organize the start-up party, she'd been on nonstop and felt in serious need of some relaxation.

It was seven. She had two hours before Christopher was going to show up.

Enough time for a shower and a glass of wine, she thought, already calming at the plans in her head. Her shower was quick, rinsing off the grime and stress of the city.

She checked her watch again. With enough time to get in some decent chilling, Sophie decided to wrap up in her coziest and oldest pajamas and take her wine to the rooftop with a blanket and a good book. The air seemed so much fresher up there, away from the fumes and the funk of the day-to-day bustle. She had every intention of spending a good hour's downtime before heading back into the warm and getting changed for Chris's arrival.

The door to the rooftop had been carelessly and thoughtlessly left ajar, allowing the chill to seep into the bones of the building. She sighed, immediately knowing who the culprit would be. Determined not to let him ruin yet another of her evenings, Sophie pushed through the door to outside.

What she saw wasn't much of a shock to her; she had witnessed Nathan in so many varying states of undress over the last year that it hardly phased her anymore.

Apart from last night. Last night was the first time she'd seen him totally naked. Her mind wandered back to that beautiful vision: the ridges of muscle on his torso, the pronounced 'V' where his hips met the top of his legs, shaped like a big arrow pointing downward to his ...

Sophie shook her head. *Stop it,* she told herself. He may have the most knicker melting body she'd ever seen, but the man was a wanker.

Noisily, she scuffed her way over to the little chair and table she had placed on top of the building before Nathan had moved in.

She wanted to let the panting bodies beneath the blanket know that she was there, and that she was not going to be moving for the next hour, not this time. If Nathan chose to have sex on a roof terrace that they both *shared,* he was damn well going to have to put up with interruptions.

Nothing.

She set her wine glass down loudly and then coughed; it was obvious that she was going to have to make her presence known in a less subtle way.

The cough did the trick. First, Nathan's head popped up from the blanket. As was typical, he was wearing nothing, at least on his top half, his bare shoulders a creamy white against the backdrop of night. Then a woman's head emerged. A different woman from the evening before, Sophie noted with disgust. If possible, this one was even more beautiful. She looked confused, frowning first at Sophie and then toward Nathan beside her.

"Hey! My favorite neighbor. Darling, this is Sophie." Nathan made his one way introductions with not an ounce of humility, shame or embarrassment. *Arsehole.* She hadn't missed that Nathan hadn't said the girl's name. Git probably didn't even know it.

"Want to come join? It's warm under here?" Nathan lifted the blanket covering him and Canada up slightly, inviting Sophie in. His female companion stared at him, openmouthed in shock, but Sophie knew better than to react in the way he wanted.

"I'd have thought this activity would have been better performed inside without the chill." Sophie muttered, staring only at the pages in her book.

"Nah, it's even more fun in the cold. A good excuse to keep warm. Plus, it's really snug over here." He paused, waiting for an answer that he didn't get. "So, are you here to watch? Because we're just going to carry on."

Was he fucking serious? Well she wasn't leaving. "You two just carry on. Don't let me disturb you."

He lifted a brow at her. "Do you like to watch, Sophie?"

She flushed. *Shit.* Had he finally remembered?

Canada reached to the floor to pick up her discarded clothing. "I should go … " she said, clearly feeling awkward by the frosty exchange between the pair. Nathan grabbed her wrist to stop her.

"No. Don't worry. We were here first. If Sophie wants to

stay, then she can stay." He stared her directly in the eye before covering the two of them back over with the throw.

Sophie adjusted her position in the chair and tried to start reading. She read the same word over and over about fifty times before finally letting out an exasperated cry and grabbing her things to head back downstairs.

Coward.

～

"WHAT THE HELL WAS THAT?" Canada whispered to Nathan, still under the makeshift tent Nathan had constructed around them.

"Ah, it's just my neighbor. She's got a problem with me. I don't know why," he answered. But suddenly he wasn't in the mood anymore. He passed Canada her clothes and coat.

"Come on. It is a little cold up here. Let's go inside. I'll call you a cab."

She looked confused but followed his lead anyway.

He hated to admit it, but Sophie had gotten into his head. He hated that every time they saw each other it involved some kind of argument. It was like the two of them were circling each other, marking their territory like neighborhood cats. He knew that he antagonized her and sometimes quite purposefully. At first, it had just been a bit of fun, a bit of teasing. He never thought that she'd continue to retaliate in such a way. And then it had formed into a habit.

Sometimes, he thought he could see a glint in her eye when she'd come over to complain. Thought that deep down perhaps it was a nice little 'in' joke the two of them had going on. But tonight had felt a lot different to that. Was something bothering her? Moreover, what the fuck did he care?

As he said goodbye to Canada, he noticed Sophie's boyfriend making the final steps to her front door. He smiled and tipped his head, being friendly to Canada. But the git just blatantly ignored him and knocked on Sophie's door.

Wow, he thought. *The two of them sure as hell suit each other.*

~

"AM I GLAD TO SEE YOU." Sophie wrapped her arms around Chris's slender frame. He pecked her on the lips quickly.

"The bloke across the hall just smiled at me. What's the deal?"

Sophie almost laughed, tired and borderline hysterical. "You honestly couldn't make that guy up. He's probably smiling because he's a smug git. He was up on the roof terrace again earlier."

"With the girl I saw leaving?" Christopher asked taking off his glasses and cleaning them on the edge of his jumper.

"Yeah. He is so arrogant; he's got no shame. Didn't care a tiny bit that I wanted to use the space, just carried on fu— with his antics." Sophie quickly edited the word 'fucking' from her sentence. Christopher was a little old-fashioned and liked his ladies to be, well, *ladies*. She hated the way he frowned whenever she swore too much, though she found his little foible cute and endearing.

In a world where men and woman were equal, as it should be, she thought, she secretly quite enjoyed his old-fashioned values: opening doors; minding his manners around her. It was a little corner of her world where she could feel different. Special, sometimes, she guessed. Okay, sometimes it made things a little … stiff between them.

She could never actually quite relax enough around him to be herself as she was sure that he'd hate the loud, brazen sass queen bubbling beneath the surface of her persona. But it worked for her nicely; they didn't spend a lot of time together and it was kinda fun to take on this slightly calmer version of herself around him. Almost like a break from herself in some ways.

"I can't get over the kinds of women he dates. I have never even looked a girl like that in the eye, let alone got one alone up on a roof terrace," Christopher mused.

What the fuck? "Uh … hello? I'm right here." Sophie pulled him up on his statement with a shake of her head. "The kinds of women Nathan dates are bimbo models without an ounce of personality. I thought there was a bit more about you than that? Anyway," she said, unable to resist a little dig, seeing as how Christopher had just been so openly, if unknowingly, rude, "it's obvious he's going to go for stunning women. Have you seen him? He's got the pick of any woman in the world, I expect. And he bloody knows it."

Her statement had the desired effect. Christopher walked over to the fridge and asked if she wanted a drink, suddenly keen to change the subject. She was glad. Arsewipe took up enough of her negative headspace as it was. She was done talking about him. So why the hell could she not shake him from her head?

"Hey." Sophie suddenly remembered. "Do you want to come to a party on New Year's? I had someone drop their plus one."

"Charming. What an invite." Christopher smiled. "Yeah sure. I'd like to come and see what keeps you so busy all the time. I am a bit miffed that we won't get to continue our tradition."

Sophie forced a smile back at him, unable to work out why she was faking it. Maybe because their New Year's Eve tradition involved consuming too much wine and him passing out before midnight. She'd never had that midnight kiss.

7

---

wo Weeks Later…
   All day, Sophie had been running around at the
bar underneath her flat, barking into her phone and trying
to get all the final loose ends tied up and ready for the
evening ahead. The bar had been a little bit of an anticli-
max. She'd been expecting something uber cool and different. Instead, it was just like any other bar she'd been to.
   Some exposed brick. Ridiculously low lighting. Some of
the seating booths were pretty neat—surrounded by loads
of plush colored chiffon sheets, giving each booth a private,
Moulin Rouge kind of feel—but other than that, it was
nothing special.
   Everything was going smoothly; the caterers had turned
up on time, the decorators had placed some tall, palm-like
fronds with some funky up-lighting beneath them around,
as well as some jungle themed waiting costumes and
brightly colored parrot motifs. It was just enough to be
within the brief without looking like a five-year-old's birth-

day. Who in their right mind combined the holidays with a jungle motif?

Sophie was just relieved beyond belief that her client hadn't requested fake lions and tigers. It was all going to plan. There were no last minute snags. But Sophie just couldn't shake the feeling of dread, sitting like a lead weight in her stomach. At first, she couldn't work it out. She was so used to organizing these kind of events— and this one was basic compared to her usual extravagant affairs— but then it dawned on her.

The worry was because of Nathan. She was dreading seeing him. They hadn't even come across each other in passing over the last fortnight. The last time they had spoken there seemed to be pure hate between them and she was terrified he was going to show her up or embarrass her in some way.

She hated this awkwardness that he had created. Sophie was now at a stage where she dreaded coming back home after work, just in case she bumped into him.

He had accepted the RSVP, but that had had the client's name on it, not hers. She was worried that he'd take one look at her there and use his good looks to manipulate the client into getting rid of the company she worked for.

Sophie had no evidence that he was really that bad a person, but he certainly didn't seem to care about anyone other than himself, so she couldn't put it past him.

If he caused any sort of bad atmosphere in the room, she was going to have no choice but to try and reason with him. If he could just be civil and courteous for one night then she could forgive him for being such an arse. Just one night; that's all she had to make it through.

NATHAN PICKED out a ripped pair of jeans and a long sleeved jumper in preparation for this evening's party. He only ever wore a suit when it was absolutely necessary, like a wedding or something. Otherwise, he ignored every dress code he'd ever read, and he'd been let in everywhere regardless.

He was only going to this thing because his step-mother, Judith had begged him to, and if she asked him to jump, he asked how high. She'd practically saved Nathan's life when she'd married his father. Most young boys would be unhappy about an interloper. But she was everything he'd needed at the time.

He wasn't some precious little mummy's boy though, not by any means. He was just really protective over her; he admired her strength and courage and tried to repay her as best he could by being a good son. *Though, I'm the worst son in the world right now.*

Nathan hadn't been to visit her in months. True to his word, he'd skipped Christmas. Opting for getting drunk with Garret in Mallorca for the holiday. But in his defense, he's sent her a lavish gift. A first edition Agatha Christie novel as well as Agatha Christie memorabilia he'd bought at auction. As a thriller writer, she'd get a kick out of those. He'd felt terrible about missing the holiday, but there was no way he would be able to look her in the eye, knowing what he knew.

He felt the now familiar stab of disgust for his dad right in the gut. It was the only feeling he got when he thought about his father these days. Networking and choosing companies to invest in was Nathan's domain. Used to be Nathan's domain.

A year ago, Nathan had told his dad he wanted no association with him or the business, and he'd told his mum he wanted to go out and find his own way in the world, to make something for himself. The latter hadn't been a complete untruth actually, though it definitely wasn't the catalyst that had caused him to try and sever ties.

His father was persistent though; he'd give him that. On average, Nathan still received at least three invites a week to represent his dad's company at award ceremonies, to do talks to kids in school about becoming successful, or, like tonight, to invest in up-and-coming start-ups. He had turned down each and every invitation since leaving, except this one.

His mum had approached him herself about tonight— Apparently the company hosting was the sister of one of his mum's friends, and she'd pleaded with him to go.

"You know that your father doesn't trust these internet start-ups. He doesn't understand apps and technology; there's no way he'll invest without some kind of feedback from you. Just go, ask about the product so that you can tell him about it in layman's terms. He trusts your judgment. He'll listen to you."

Nathan had sighed. "I'll go if it will help out someone

you know. I'll email you the feedback and projections and you can give it to him, though. Deal?"

Now it was his mother's turn to sigh. "Oh, Nathan, I don't know what on earth's happened between the two of you. It hurts me to see you putting so much distance between you. You used to be so close."

"Until I realized that ... " Nathan stopped himself. This wasn't his job. "Dad knows exactly why. He should tell you." He imagined his mum on the other end of the phone, rubbing her eyes in exasperation. He didn't like the image. It made him feel confused about whether he was doing the right thing. It made him feel guilty for not being there.

"I'll see you soon, okay?" *Liar.*

He couldn't keep avoiding her. And he couldn't tell her either. One way or another this needed to end.

8

Every passing minute filled Sophie with more and more trepidation. With every group of guests that entered the bar, the tightly wound spring inside her coiled ever tighter as she waited for Nathan's arrival.

"Wow. You get paid to do this?" Christopher came up to her at the bar, swigging on a glass of free champagne, eyes boggling at the scantily clad waiting staff and even more scantily clad female guests. Weather be damned, the theme was sexy.

"Er, well .... yeah. Except I can't relax and get pissed like everyone else." Christopher raised his eyebrows, looking pointedly at the half empty glass of bubbles she was holding.

It made Sophie laugh. "I can have a drink or two, obviously. I need to look like I'm enjoying myself as I'm forcing enjoyment on others. But it's hardly relaxing."

"So, are you always this on edge at events? You haven't stopped looking around the room. Isn't everything in place now? Or are you just waiting for something to go wrong?"

Suddenly, Sophie wished that she'd never mentioned this evening to Christopher. He was irritating her with all his questions. Questions that she couldn't really reply to. It wasn't as if she could say, *"I'm normally really chilled out once an event gets going. But Nathan the nympho neighbor is coming to this one, and I feel really anxious about him being here for reasons that, even for me, seem slightly irrational."* Instead, she just gave him a tight smile and tried to drop her shoulders to adopt a calmer posture.

She needn't have bothered; Christopher wasn't paying her the slightest bit of attention. Momentarily, she was drawn away from her obsessing over the door to feel a bit put out.

"Stop gawping at people," she said to him in a loud whisper. She felt mean as soon as she'd said it. The people here, they weren't the sort that she and Christopher would usually be mingling with on a rare night down their local.

The bodies Sophie had hired were mostly models, and with that (combined with the rest of the guest list being representatives for some of the most successful businesses in the UK), the crowd made for a jaw-dropping bunch. Sophie was used to it now—the sheer … expensiveness that these people exuded. But Chris, this was a whole new world for Chris, coming from just as humble beginnings as her own.

"Okay." She gave him the kindest smile she could muster and rubbed his arm affectionately. "You go and mingle if you want. I just need to make sure all the canapés are going to be out on time and that the DJ's ready, then I'll be able to take more of a back seat."

It seemed that Christopher didn't need asking twice. He kissed her quickly on the cheek and then sauntered off into the darkness of the bar.

The darkness of the bar. The smoke machine obscuring the air with its scented fog ... Sophie screwed up her face and waved it away.

"Fancy meeting you here." The deep voice made her snap her eyes open, though she hadn't needed to open them to know who it belonged to.

Standing right in front of her was Nathan. And he looked so gorgeous she thought she might lick him.

~

AT FIRST, Nathan couldn't decide if Sophie was going to slap him or burst into tears. God, he hadn't ticked her off that badly, had he? She kind of wilted with disappointment when she first opened her eyes. He was not used to having that effect on a woman, that was for sure.

For the first time ever, in his life, Nathan was at a complete loss for words. Considering himself the absolute expert on reading people and being able to win them over, he found that no matter how hard he tried, he could not work out this confusing creature before him. He looked into her eyes, noticing those green flecks again, despite the dim lighting in the room, and tried to read what she was thinking. She stared right back at him, an expression on her face like ... It was so frustrating. He just didn't know.

"I'm working. This is my night, I'm the events manager," Sophie said finally. Nathan thought it might have been the most personal and pleasant conversation he'd ever had with her, even if they were only one sentence in. He liked it. He wanted to get to know her. She fascinated him, but before he could make any kind of remark back or compliment her on her good job, she interrupted.

"I don't know why you've been invited and it's not my business to know, but I'm asking you please not to discuss our ... challenging accommodation relationship with anybody here. Please."

Nathan laughed. He couldn't believe she'd thought she even had to ask him that. Who did she think he was? Of course he wouldn't talk about that here—He wouldn't talk about it to anybody she knew. Did she really think that he'd make her look bad or unprofessional? This was silly. He shook his head as his laughter died down. They really had to get to know each other better.

"Okay. Fine," Sophie said sadly, walking away before he'd even had the opportunity to talk. What the hell was that girl's problem with him? He went over to the bar and ordered a drink, feeling more than a little confused, and he didn't like it one bit.

~

SOPHIE COULDN'T BELIEVE that Nathan had just laughed in her face when she'd asked him not to talk to anyone about the kind of interaction they'd had. She stalked around the room, checking in with her client and hurrying the caterers along,

not thinking about a single thing that came out of her mouth
or listening to anything anyone was saying. Her mind was just
reeling, replaying Nathan's mockery of her over and over. She
felt hurt, bizarrely, that he hadn't afforded her some respite.

Sophie watched him draw a long sip of beer, and then
turn and smile brightly at the woman who approached him.
One of the models she had hired, no doubt. Before she
knew it, she was narrowing her eyes. And then she caught
herself.

Oh my God, Sophie. You're jealous, she thought with
shock. *No. No, I'm not jealous. I don't like him ... I can't. I don't
actually even like him as a person. Do I?*

She realized that she didn't know one single thing about
him and so, technically, she couldn't really make that
judgment.

What she did know was that she could see the way his
bicep swelled as he raised his arm to drink. She did know
that his jeans and jumper were a refreshing and sexy
change from the onslaught of suits in the bar. And she did
know the delights of that body beneath that very T-shirt.

She had also noticed that his eyes—a sunnier blue than
the turquoise oceans of the Maldives—always seemed to be
smiling. Like he was permanently happy. His confidence
knew no bounds and was sometimes quite enviable, even
inspirational to some, she guessed. She imagined he could
be quite a compelling person to be around, even without his
perfectly styled dark hair and Calvin Klein model jawline.

Sophie bit her lip, knowing full well that she had just
unleashed an entire can of worms into her head. She was

working, with her boyfriend, yet standing here thinking about how generally sexy her neighbor was. The guy who hated her guts.

Come on. You must be ill. The guy's a womanizer. He's not your thing at all. Focus, Sophie. Come back to the room. Trying to gain control of her head, she set off in search of Christopher.

Half an hour later, she made it back to the bar and eagerly grabbed a glass of champagne that was freshly poured and offered to her. She hadn't managed to find her boyfriend. Her client had instead insisted on thanking her, which was very kind, but had then introduced her to about fifteen different people. None of whom she could remember now.

As she drained her glass, one of the waitresses came up and tapped her on the shoulder.

"Excuse me. This is kind of awkward—just ... I saw you two kiss at the start of the evening and, well ... Isn't that your boyfriend over there?" She pointed in the direction of a darkened corner near the bar, murmured that she was sorry and walked away.

Sophie squinted toward where the waitress had gestured to. The light in here was so bad, but she could just about make out ...

She froze. Now that she'd located him, there was no mistaking it. Christopher was standing in front of one of the guests, a striking blond-haired beauty, and he was trying—to the point of assault—to kiss her. She was laughing shyly but it was obvious that she was trying to push him away politely. Sophie stared in horror as he lunged at the poor girl yet again.

"What the fuck?" Nathan was suddenly beside her, looking in the same direction. "That's your bloke?"

Sophie looked up at him, not bothering to hide the hurt in her eyes, and nodded. Of all the people to be witness to this, of course it was bloody Nathan. She was beyond caring anymore.

"Son of a bitch," Nathan hissed, taking a stride over toward the corner. Sophie grabbed his arm quickly.

"Don't," she said, keeping her hand on his arm. "Just leave it. I'll handle it."

"Let me see to him." Nathan's jaw was clenched tightly. Sophie could practically feel the anger pouring from him. How bizarre that the whole time she'd known him, she'd seen nothing but arrogance and ignorance, yet now here he was, by her side wanting to fight for her honor. If she wasn't feeling so crushed by the scene in front of her, she'd have almost enjoyed having a knight in shining armor.

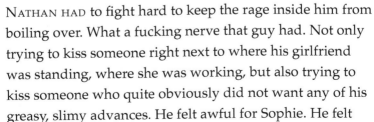

NATHAN HAD to fight hard to keep the rage inside him from boiling over. What a fucking nerve that guy had. Not only trying to kiss someone right next to where his girlfriend was standing, where she was working, but also trying to kiss someone who quite obviously did not want any of his greasy, slimy advances. He felt awful for Sophie. He felt furious with that dick of a guy.

Had Sophie not touched his arm just then, he would've

gone over and knocked the guy to the floor. It was the least he deserved.

He watched with curiosity as Sophie gently pulled Christopher away from the woman and saw her whisper in his ear. Christopher put his hands in his face, clearly ashamed. Nathan hoped to God that Sophie wasn't going to go easy on him. He was willing her to slap him in the face or kick him in the balls. Anything to cause him the pain he should be feeling right now.

But instead she just walked slowly with him to the door and he saw her mouth goodbye to him. Nathan was stunned. How had she managed to keep her composure that well?

If he thought that it wouldn't show her up, he'd have given her a round of applause for keeping her head together during all that.

9

———————

"Get out," she hissed through clenched teeth. It was all she was able to say, given the circumstances. It wasn't like she could exactly have a full-blown meltdown in the middle of work. And she was too strong for that. The only way that Sophie could get through it was to try and shut out the feelings. For now, at least. But she did allow herself one long, deep breath after closing the door behind Chris's lying, cheating, model shagging arse.

Christopher scrubbed his hands over his face. "Fuck Sophie. I'm pissed. I'm sorry."

She could only stare at him. What the fuck had just happened? She'd spent the last two years of her life with that wanker. She'd even changed her hair for him. And he offered no explanation other than he'd had too much to drink?

"Two choices. You can leave now, or I can have you put out. You choose." She turned from him, unable to meet his gaze again. She just wanted him out of her face. She just prayed that he would choose option one.

She just couldn't make sense of what she'd just witnessed. Christopher had been trying it on with another woman. In *front* of the people she worked with.

What the hell was wrong with her that she—Oh God. Her stomach clenched. Nathan had seen that. Mr. Smug Bastard himself.

Of course, he'd been there to see that, Sophie thought bitterly, heat suffusing her face. Because what good was public humiliation unless your nemesis was there to witness it? With her luck, he probably recorded the whole thing for Photogram or something. Not that she secretly stalked him on social media under a pseudonym like @neighbourswhostalk, because that would be creepy …

Humiliation twisted her insides. Christopher was not the kind of boyfriend to cheat. She was supposed to be able to count on him.

Swallowing back the tears, she dug her nails into her palm. She could get through the rest of the night. Independent woman and all that. Also, she had a tub of cookie dough ice cream waiting in her freezer at home and several bottles of wine. That was her motivation. If she was a good girl, she could just stuff and drown her feelings with ice cream and alcohol. A regular chip off the old block. There were only a few hours left to go. Only then could she break down. Not before.

Plastering a smile back on to her face, she forced her way through the throngs of people, hoping to God that she looked a damn sight more cheerful than she felt.

But her mind was reeling. How the hell had she been so wrong? About him, about everything? She'd been a good girlfriend, right? She'd been accommodating. Down to coloring her hair blond and always wearing it up. He'd always said she looked messy and unkempt with it down. And he said her natural red hair made her look like a tart.

Why had she been with him again? Oh right. Because he'd been steady. Dependable ... Well, so much for that.

God. Nathan had seen that.

Wait.

Sophie suddenly remembered the look in Nathan's eye as he had clocked what Christopher was doing. She'd had to hold him back. Had he been ready to fight him? *For her?* But that couldn't be right. Nathan was a prick. He didn't care about anything.

No.

That is not true. He'd wanted to stand up for her. No matter how she tried to play the scenario back in her head, there was simply no denying the fact that Nathan had been in her corner as she was being publicly humiliated. That went against the whole nature of their relationship.

Fuck, she couldn't process any of that right now. She didn't understand why her heart was pounding out of her chest thinking about it. She wanted to feel that blissfully numb feeling of someone who has had a lot of wine. But thinking about what Nathan had tried to do for her made her feel hot and breathless.

For the next hour, she tried her hardest to convince herself that she was just functioning as normal, checking on the event, making sure everybody was doing their jobs properly. But after an hour of running herself ragged to avoid thinking, she gave in, and admitted to herself that what she was really doing was looking for Nathan.

Bizarrely, the only person she wanted to see at that moment was him, though she wasn't sure why. He had made her feel safe somehow, just by being willing to defend her.

She searched the sea of faces before her, almost in desperation. But he was nowhere to be found.

With an inexplicably heavy heart, she realized he must have left. It pinched when it dawned on her that he wouldn't have left alone. Of course he wouldn't. It was stupid to even want to see him. It was pathetic to want the ... ego stroke. *Yeah, ego ... That's what we'll call it.*

What do you care? she admonished herself. *You can't stand the guy and you full well know what he's like.* Why would he have waited around for her, with the amount of smoking hot women in here?

Her mind's attempt at rationalization was lackluster at best, but she refused to look any closer at her feelings. The night had already been shitty. She didn't need to compound it with thinking about Mr. Dirty.

Suddenly, a blanket of desperation and loneliness wrapped around her. She was sick to death of being let down. Even when deliberately choosing right, she still chose wrong. What the hell was the point?

"I am literally the worst judge of character," she laughed as she passed through the crowd, not entirely sure of the direction she was heading. She was grateful that the volume of the music drowned her out.

After another painful two hours, the night ground slowly to a close. As the guests began filtering out, her impatience increased. Forcing a smile and a jovial mood was bloody tiring, especially when all she wanted to do was fling a duvet over her head and sob.

Finally, once the client had again gushed her thank yous, Sophie was left alone but for the staff of the bar. Having had one of the most emotionally fraught evenings of her work life so far, she faked cheerful goodbyes to those left, and with a relief so great it made her shoulders sag, she mounted the stairs up to her flat, planning on shutting the door and hiding in there forever.

So much for a great New Year's Eve.

Outside her door, however, was a sight she hadn't been expecting to see. Nathan leaning against her door ... waiting.

Her first thought, as was always her first thought when she saw him, was *Goddamn.* There was no way that she would ever get over being in front of someone who looked that good in real life. It was disconcerting. As always, she was drawn to his eyes first; that cerulean gaze hypnotized her like a stormy sea. Almost unconsciously, her gaze fell to his body.

It was only then that she realized he was holding an expensive bottle of champagne in one hand and two glasses in the other. She stopped dead on the top step, gawking at him, wondering what in the hell was going on. *What is he doing?* Was he having a party? She really couldn't deal with that right now. Frustrated, she tugged her hair our of the bun and shook it out.

"Look, I'm not in the mood to be fucked with right now."

"I figured after the night you've just had, you might need a drink?" He held the bottle aloft. "Rooftop?"

~

THE LOOK on Sophie's face was a mixture of surprise and wariness. Not that he could blame her.

"Why?"

"Because you look like you need it."

He'd left quickly after she'd seen her boyfriend out. He didn't know how long she'd be forced to stay and work, but he'd wanted to do something to make her feel better.

Fuck him, he was going soft.

After watching her deal with that, Nathan had developed a newfound admiration for uptight Sophie. But it wasn't just that. Not if he was being completely honest. It was the way she'd handled herself. She was literally the soul of that party, making sure everyone had a good time. She did her job despite her mood. Would he have been able to do that? Probably not.

She ran a hand through her hair and his brain tried to follow the thread of recognition, but it snapped in an instant.

Sophie stuttered, clearly not quite sure what to make of his offer. He couldn't help but laugh out loud when he heard her. "You don't even like me."

"Don't look so suspicious. I'm only suggesting a drink. I

know I usually go up there with my dates, but I promise you, I only want to cheer you up."

She barked a laugh. "I didn't think that. I know I'm not your type.

He frowned. "What's my type?"

"Supermodel perfection." She shook her head. "I've had a rough night and I'm tired … "

"Oh, come on. It's only a drink. You fucking deserve it after tonight." He wasn't going to take no for an answer. Regardless of their somewhat unfriendly history, he couldn't bear the thought that she might sit in her flat alone and cry over that twat. He held her eyes with a steely gaze, not backing down.

Her body relented before she spoke, moving toward him despite her obvious reservations. "Okay. Thanks. I really bloody need a drink."

It was the first time they'd ever had a pleasant exchange.

He grinned at her, thinking how nice she looked when she smiled. He still thought she was uptight, but he could begin to see the chinks of the person beneath that wound tight veneer.

Up on the roof, he pointed to one of the chairs. "Sit down," he instructed, pouring champagne into both of the glasses. Sophie downed it straight away and then exhaled deeply, puffing her cheeks out.

"I have to tell you, I was disappointed you didn't let me knock that wanker the fuck out. I hope you gave him what for before he left."

Sophie shook her head sadly. "Honestly? I'd love to tell you I did, but pathetically, I just told him to go." She turned to look at him. "I think all the fight's gone out of me now. I'm fucked off with men. I'm fucked off with being led on. I just want one goddamn bloke to actually be who he says he is, not sell me some lie about commitment." Her head dropped and she stared at the floor. "I'm so done with it all."

Nathan sipped his drink. "Don't let that wanker get the best of you. You're looking at this all wrong."

Sophie glanced up at him, her brow furrowing.

"Being done can be a good thing," he said. "Go out, meet people, have your fun and engage in nothing emotionally. You can put your focus on other things, if you want, but you don't have to become the Virgin Mary. It just means that you don't have to put up with other people's bullshit anymore." He laughed at her expression.

She was beautiful on another level from the women who he usually spent his time with. They were usually carbon copies of empty perfection. Sophie was much less polished, less put together, but there was a natural prettiness that seemed to shine from her. She didn't cover her freckles or freak out that she wasn't perfect. She was real.

"Nathan. Are you trying to convince me that if I became the female version of you I'd be happier?"

He noticed that she always had a lilt in her tone, like everything she was saying had sarcastic undertones. It made her sound sharp and sassy. He liked it.

He shrugged his shoulders. "Yeah. That's exactly what I'm suggesting. I'm happy. I have lots of company, I get lots of sex … "

"Don't I bloody know it," Sophie said, snorting.

"I'm trying to help you here." He swiveled in the chair so that he was facing her. "I can show you. I can be like your guide in the quest for … "

"For an STD?" She laughed.

The laugh sputtered out of him. It was that very sauciness that he found utterly compelling. She wasn't into any bullshit; she just said things as they were. It was refreshing.

"I was going to say for emotional freedom." He cringed at the phrase as soon as it was out of his mouth. "All right, that sounds crap. But there's a skill—it can't be cold, emotionless encounters. Shagging people like they don't matter is going to make you feel more shit. It's about controlling your emotions, being in control and most importantly … " He paused for dramatic effect, wanting to make his point. " … being honest."

Sophie blinked at him for a couple of seconds before shaking her head with a smile. "You know what, I am too tired and drained to argue with you on this, so while you've got me at my most vulnerable, I'm just going to say okay. You're on. Show me your ways, oh Sex Yoda."

Fuck, she was so sharp and switched on, and … sexy. She had some sort of spark about her that he was enjoying being on the receiving end of. She was challenging and bright. *Intriguing.* And with her hair wild and flowing around her, he was once again struck by the sense of familiarity.

He fought the pull. He didn't want this. He'd invited her for a drink out because he felt bad for her. She wasn't even his type. *But you want her.* And here he was now.

He shook the thought. "Right. We start tomorrow night.

Your first lesson, young student." Nathan clinked the side of her glass.

"So enough about me now. What about you? I know exactly nothing about you, other than from your public shagging tendencies. And in one night you've already learned my job and both my relationship status and relationship goals. You have to tell me at least something, so that it's even."

The change in direction had his grin stiffening. He'd spent most of his life trying to keep things light. Nothing too deep. But she was right. She needed a quid pro quo. He cleared his throat, wondering where on earth to start. When was the last time he'd had a revealing conversation about himself?

He was silent too long because she gave him a sad smile and an easy out. "Look, I'm shattered," Sophie said, putting down her glass and throwing the blanket from her lap. "Why don't you save your story to tell me during 'class' tomorrow?"

It was obvious that Sophie had noticed the shift in him and had decided to change the subject. While relieved, a part of him want to share *something*.

It wasn't that he was hiding who he was exactly, but he liked this version of Sophie. And he knew how people changed the moment they heard his last name. For now, for as long as he could, he wanted Sophie to just judge him on what she knew. *Are you sure about that?* Like she had before when they'd done nothing but argue.

As uncomfortable and irritating as that may have been, at least he knew it was real.

10

_____

When her feet hit the landing, Sophie knew that as soon as she said goodbye to him her mind would be reeling with everything that had happened that night. She felt like she'd been awake for a week and so far, she hadn't had even a second to process any of it.

"Do you want to keep the champagne?" Nathan asked, offering her what was left of the bottle.

Sophie stared at it for a second, thinking. She only had one measly beer in her fridge. Hard to drink herself to sleep with just a beer. She didn't even like beer.

"Yeah, why not?" She reached out for the bottle to take it from him. Her hand brushed against his in the exchange and, she didn't know if it was her exhaustion or what, but the accidental touch made her body mutiny.

A spark shot through her, so powerful that it almost made her jump. Heat crept up her neck and to her cheeks, and she knew damn well that she would be an obvious, beetroot red. Her breath quickened, even as her clearly confused nipples hardened into tight, little points. *Shit*. The last thing she needed tonight was an attack of the lady bits.

She'd been so down earlier that she'd hadn't cared about what he thought. But she was hyperaware of him now, feeling flustered and unable to look him in the eye. "Thanks," she whispered, cursing herself for turning to mush. Cursing him for having that effect on her. *You touched his hand. For crying out loud, get a grip.*

She snatched the bottle out of his hand far too quickly. And it flew out of her grasp and up into the air.

Everything seemed to move in slow motion. Sophie and Nathan watched as the bottle spun above her head, showering them both in sticky liquid, before plummeting back down toward the ground.

Nathan moved like lightning, practically lifting a frozen-in-shock Sophie up, and moving her to the side, just as the bottle crashed at their feet and smashed into pieces.

There was a pause as they both silently looked at the carnage beneath them and then simultaneously, up at each other.

The hysterical laugh bubble up uncontrollably at the sight of the perfect man in front of her dripping with remnants of champagne.

And then she humiliated herself and began to cry. Because it wasn't already shitty enough. It was as though all her emotions were just pouring out; she was powerless to stop them. Between sobs she laughed, not quite sure whether she was coming or going.

That smashed bottle, the smell of fizz in her hair—it was just the cherry on the top of her fucking cake tonight.

Nathan didn't hesitate. He put his hand on her arm. His touch was firm and reassuring. "Hey. Hey," he said softly. "There's no point in crying over spilled champagne."

Sophie laughed again, once, before more tears came. *I'm going fucking mad*, she thought, completely unable to control herself. Then, Nathan ran his fingers down the side of her cheek, brushing away some of the splashes.

Both her hysterics and sobbing abruptly stopped. *Hello again, lady bits.*

His touch was softer than she had anticipated. If she had been in her right mind, she would have even described it as tender. But she was definitely not in her right mind. She looked up at him, feeling overwhelmed and confused.

He trailed a path down her cheek to her chin, where his fingers rested lightly. Sophie forgot how to breathe. There was no mistaking the look in his eyes.

There were no need for words. *Oh my God, he's going to kiss me.*

Amidst all that had happened, as soon as the intention behind his look became obvious to her, her insides began to melt. A swarm of butterflies burst in her belly as they continued to gaze at each other.

Nathan dipped his head slightly before stopping and scanning over her face as if checking for permission. Involuntarily, Sophie's lips parted.

She was close enough to see the shining gold of the dark stubble covering his jawline. He smelled like musk and ocean her wildest fantasy.

God, please kiss me. Every heartbeat sent a violent throb between her legs as the anticipation of having Nathan Windsor this close to her began to take over her most primal instincts.

Finally, Nathan tilted her chin upwards and, with his gaze unfaltering, met her lips with his.

His mouth was hot, unbelievably soft and slightly sticky from the champagne. He gently flicked his tongue along her bottom lip teasingly slowly, before kissing her harder, his mouth firmly and passionately on hers.

Sliding both hands around the small of her back, he tugged her into him. Her body pressed hard up against the firmness of his and she couldn't help but push in further, wanting every single part of her sliding against him, wanting every part of him touching her.

If he hadn't been holding her so strongly, she was sure that her knees would have buckled and she would have fallen to the floor. There was not one single point in her life where she could remember ever feeling like she wanted someone this badly. Her head was swimming.

"Jesus, you are so damn sexy. Why do you taste so good?" Nathan murmured, his words vibrating against her lips, his breath hot against her lips. It felt naughty and sensual.

Hearing him say that she was turning him on made her moan softly. Instinctively, she canted her pelvis against him, her body moving independently of her mind. She needed him so bad.

Nathan's hand slid to her hips, tightening, and he groaned low as he pulled her against the length of his pulsing erection. The impact of her pelvic bone hitting his thigh lit a firework in her clitoris. She felt it pulse and begin to swell.

He moved his mouth to the edge of her earlobe. "I really want to know what you taste like everywhere. Right here in your neck. On your belly. Right behind your knee. And Jesus, I really want to know what your pussy tastes like," he whispered. This time, Sophie's knees did buckle, though Nathan's grip was tight enough to steady her.

His voice seemed to travel directly to her clit, each word massaging the growing ball of heat gathering there. He bit her earlobe and she erupted in pleasurable goose bumps, the sweet pain tickling down her spine like an electric current.

What the fuck was happening here? Sophie was just about ready to rip her clothes off and scream at him to take her when a seed of self-doubt trickled in.

What the hell is he doing kissing me? I'm not a supermodel; I'm not his normal type. Goddamn, am I about to be a pity fuck?

She swallowed and stilled. Once the thought had been let loose her buzz immediately died. Nathan could have the pick of any girl he wanted. He was the fittest man she'd ever seen. *Ever.* He was self-assured and intimidatingly confident. Why on earth was he kissing her?

Sensing her stiffness, Nathan pulled away and held her at arm's length. "You okay?" he asked, his voice soft.

She shuffled, horny to the point of desperation and instantly regretting the thoughts in her head. Straight away, she wanted him to kiss her again. She needed him to touch her. But there was no way she was getting a pity fuck. Even at this point, so turned on she might explode, she had some self-respect. *Yeah right. Is that why you want to rub up against him like an alley cat?*

"It's not that ... I mean...I want to ... " She tried to get the words out and failed. She wanted to tell him that she wanted him to fuck her like she'd never wanted anything before, but she was too terrified. The words wouldn't come out.

Nathan shrugged, like it was no bother to him. Like nothing ever was. *What must it feel like to have absolutely no worries?* Sophie pondered.

"You want to come into mine?" he offered casually. Sophie's heart began racing again.

"No. Thanks, I'd better ... " *What? What are you doing?* she screamed inside. *This total GOD is inviting you in to possibly give you the fuck of your entire life, and you're having self-esteem issues?*

"Your call. Guess it's a cold shower for me, then."

Of course that only drew her attention to his massive erection. Sophie's gaze drifted down his body and watched with hunger as the bulge behind his jeans pulsed. Oh hell. She licked her lips, wondering if she would regret this moment for the rest of her life.

IT WAS CERTAINLY a rare occasion when Nathan got turned down by a woman. And it made something deep and visceral only want her more. But he recognized it as the urge to chase. *Hell no.* He shut that shit down. He'd survive an empty bed for the night.

Sure his cock wanted to jump out and plead with her to touch him, but Sophie had more than good reason; she had just seen her boyfriend try to kiss another girl right in front of her face and then had had to carry on smiling. It had been a rough night for her.

He'd had no intention of kissing her when he'd offered champagne and an ear. Yes, he'd found her composure compelling tonight, and all right, she'd looked well fit too, but seducing her had genuinely not been his game plan.

She'd just been standing there looking lost and vulnerable with champagne dripping from the ends of her hair and he'd wanted to taste her. *Yeah, next time, think that through, mate.* Laughing like a mad woman with tears streaming down her face, she'd been so exposed, so raw … so beautiful.

He'd never seen somebody as honest and as real as that. Not close-up. It was a privileged thing, to witness somebody's emotions in that way, *especially as we barely know each other*, he thought.

He felt as though he had seen every single part of Sophie's personality laid bare, and it was the innocence and honesty that he'd found so attractive. She'd been unable to hide anything from him in that moment and he'd seen that she was a good person, right down to the core.

And then he'd been slammed with a sledgehammer that was recognition. He suddenly knew why she seemed so familiar. Her hair was different but she was the redhead from the party a year ago.

His whole life, all he'd witnessed were people lying to each other about who they really were. The one reason he hadn't been fucked up about his past was because of his dad, and now the one man he'd looked up to as his inspiration had blown that all to shit.

Until tonight, he hadn't thought he would ever trust someone fully again. Until tonight, he was of the opinion that deep down, everyone was capable of being mistrustful and a lying dick. Until he'd seen Sophie and discovered that, just maybe, his conclusion of the human race didn't apply to absolutely *everybody*.

It was a daunting thought, and he didn't want to dwell on it too long. The urge to kiss her had just come over him, and goddamn he was glad it had. Because now he knew why she'd always seemed so familiar.

Clearly she didn't recognize him. But he knew her all right. Her eyes had haunted him for a year.

Nathan knew that the desire to fuck somebody was what bullshitters described as a 'spark.' Now, much to his bewilderment, he thought he could kind of see what these people were talking about.

He fucking hadn't recognized her. *How?* Hell, he had wanted to fuck her all right, from the minute he'd seen her downstairs looking aloof, but when he'd kissed her, it had been different. Deeper. *More ...*

I really need to take care of this. Nathan directed his thoughts toward his throbbing hard dick. *It's fucking with my head, clearly.*

Being horny for too long was obviously making him think bullshit, so he grabbed his laptop and headed into his bedroom to resolve the issue. Maybe after, he could forget all this crap about sparks and get his head back in to focus. He fucking hoped so. So what if she was the girl from the bar? So what if he'd thought about her for the better part of a year? He was *not fucked*.

11

It was a struggle for Sophie to think of anything other than that kiss. Though she'd been beyond exhaustion the night before, sleep had been replaced by the continual replay of Nathan kissing her. Each time she relived it, the tingle low in her belly flared and no amount of wishing it away would stop it.

She rolled over and grabbed her phone, scrolling through her messages and all the while refusing to leave the security of her duvet. Fuck, so much had changed in just twelve hours. There were five missed calls from Chris, as well as multiple text messages. She ignored them all.

The stab of hurt in her stomach was quick and swift when she thought of the humiliation of last night. But just as quickly as her stomach cramped, the pain was instantly replaced by butterflies low in her belly.

Yeah ... That's not your belly.

Okay, fine. Somewhere in the *vicinity* of her belly. If she was being honest, the fluttering was happening a good deal more south of her belly, but details.

The image of Christopher kissing that other woman hurt. *Does it really?* She shoved the question aside. Of course it hurt. *Does it hurt or are you more embarrassed?*

That kiss with Nathan canceled out the hurt, though. She groaned and tossed in the bed. The problem was her subconscious was a good deal less shocked and hurt by what had happened than her heart was.

Deep down she'd always known Christopher had been filler. A good solid guy who bored her stiff. She'd been trying to make herself love him. But if she was honest, what they had wasn't love. It was a standing twice a week dinner arrangement followed by a mediocre shag that never resulted in an orgasm for her unless she helped herself along … which of course made him feel insufficient.

She'd eventually had to stop assisting herself to orgasm when he was done because all he'd do was moan and whinge about why she had to do that. And how emasculated he felt. So there had gone her little spot of happy. She shook her head. There were much better things to think about.

Not for the first time, Sophie buried her head in her pillow as she recalled, once again, how she'd ended it with Nathan. She got it now. The endless stream of women. When he wasn't being an arse, he was sweet. Couple that with his charm and that smile, hell she'd been so tempted.

I should have just gone into his place. I'm such an idiot.

Why had she panicked? Yes, Nathan was a dirty man whore, which was part of the appeal. He clearly knew how to deliver an orgasm. More than likely multiple ones. Hell, just a little bit of dirty talk from his smooth as silk voice and she'd been halfway there last night.

You could have been making up for the lack of orgasms over the last year.

Instead, she lay in bed admonishing herself. Why had she let the thought of just how many women he'd slept with ruin everything? *Because you want to be wanted for you. You want to feel special.* But Nathan certainly wasn't the make you feel special forever guy. He was the make you feel special *right now* guy. And right now, that was what she needed.

The memory of him holding her so strongly, kissing her like she was the only woman on earth, was so burned into her mind that she could still smell him.

She groaned again and rolled over. This wasn't fair. Why was he so damn nice? He had told her that he was going to take her out tonight, to show her how to have fun without having the heartache, apparently. *Will we still be going?* She worried that she might have put him off her completely. He probably thought that she was far too much of an emotional wreck, probably a liability. He surely wouldn't want to hang out with her now? She wouldn't blame him.

No, no, no. *Enough men.* Enough getting involved.

Sophie threw off her blankets and got out of bed with a new, determined resolution. Nathan was not the sort of guy she was looking for. Too good looking. Too much of a player. In fact, he was the very opposite of the kind of guy she wanted. So they'd kissed. So what? She tried to gain control of her thoughts. She meant what she'd told him last night. She *was* done with men. She was done with being treated like shit and taken for a mug.

Her interest in Nathan was purely physical. The man was a freaking sex god, if the moans she heard from his flat were to be believed. There was no way she was going to be able to overlook that, but he wasn't the kind of person she needed in her life romantically.

So she figured she'd let him instruct her in his ways, teach her how to meet guys without getting attached and surely after a while, she'd become used to his hotness. No more dwelling on that kiss. *No more regretting that it didn't lead to sex because she'd turned him down.*

How he'd been last night had surprised her, to say the least. Once she'd pushed his lips from her mind, she was left with curious intrigue. She'd been wrong about him. Or at the very least she hadn't had the whole picture. Guilt wormed its way into her heart.

Yes, the man was a walking, talking orgasm and he had a lot of female company. But maybe the reason she'd always loathed him had nothing to do with him at all. Maybe it was because she saw the appeal and hated it. Hated that she was weak. Just like every other female on the planet, she recognized the alpha male and she wanted some of what he had to offer.

So much for being a feminist.

Shit, did she even know what that was? Yes, he was a total pain in the arse, but he also had a heart hiding in there under all those pheromones. And she felt a little guilty as she remembered how cold she'd been toward him.

Last night, he'd been really sweet. He'd stood up for her,

tried to cheer her up. Then he'd kissed her and promised her body an orgasm so good she might become an addict. *No. Do not think about that.*

Last night, Nathan had been there for her, even though she'd thought their dislike of each other was mutual. If he hadn't have been there, if he hadn't met her and offered a friendly drink, she knew she'd have spent the entire night crying. It was time to admit that she just may have been wrong about him.

12

——————

Nathan woke with a smile ... and a hard-on. *Thank you, Sophie*. Apparently, the cold shower last night hadn't helped. Nor had the two times he'd jerked himself off just thinking about her tongue sliding over his.

Careful, he warned himself. This was unfamiliar territory. He didn't dwell on women. That was a habit that didn't get him anywhere. So why her? He'd kissed quite possibly well over a hundred women. But one taste of neighbor Sophie and his damned dick was on mutiny? He knew himself well enough to be wary of the newfound fondness he had for his neighbor. His parents had well and truly put him off of meaningful connections for the rest of his life.

After another quick, cold shower that didn't seem to work, he grabbed his laptop and quickly checked his email, throwing himself into his work with gusto. While he may be the product of a man who had taught him that relationships could dissolve to nothing and be based on lies and deception, the old man had also taught him that hard work could reap rewards that felt sturdier and more fulfilling than devoting your heart and affections to someone who would, ultimately, throw it back in your face.

Pretend all you want. You are your father's son.

He managed to pass the rest of the day without one thought about Sophie. Okay, maybe one or two, but he'd successfully shut them down hard. However, the moment he shut his laptop, she was the first thing that popped into his head and she didn't leave. And hello permanent hard-on once again.

It's just because I'm supposed to be coaching her tonight, he reassured himself. Once he'd set her on the right track, once he'd helped her to protect herself from wankers in the future, he would be able to get himself back in the zone. Back to his phone book of fun. He smiled, excited about his little project with her.

LATER THAT NIGHT, at seven, Nathan crossed the hallway and knocked hard on her door. "Turn that bloody music down," he joked when she answered.

Sophie grinned and then frowned. "What are you doing here so early? I haven't even showered yet."

Nathan barged past her and into her flat. He walked into the middle of her lounge and looked around. The more normal he acted, the sooner they could both forget that he knew how she tasted. "I think my place might be bigger than yours," he observed casually.

Sophie shook her head as she followed him. "Of course. You have the big one."

"That's what she said." Nathan laughed at her unintended pun, not caring if she thought it was immature. She rolled her eyes, but there was a smile playing on her lips.

"Stop it," she warned. "You have the bigger flat because I would have to work ten jobs to afford that one. Besides, this one is huge. Far too huge for one person to live in really." A frown crossed her face briefly. "What is it that you do again? How come you can afford that place just for you to rattle around in? No wonder you have so much company over."

He chose to ignore her first questions and simply answer her statement. There would be plenty of time for him to talk about himself later.

"You'll have plenty of company here soon. I'm ready to train you for *Operation Good Times*. Now, get yourself in the shower. I've come early on purpose. The change of attitude starts before we even go out, so I'm here to psyche you up for it."

She opened her mouth as if to argue and then it seemed she thought better of it. "So I guess we're really doing this, huh?"

Nathan took her shoulders, spun her around and gave her a gentle push in the direction of her bathroom. "We are. Now go and get ready."

As she closed the door behind her, he tried to banish the

image of her wet, naked body, just a wall away from where he was standing. Never mind the fact that he'd been staring at her lips the whole time they'd been talking, that kiss not as far from his mind as it should have been. And he really wanted to know if she remembered him too.

13

———

Sophie felt the eyes of every single woman in the bar fall upon her. Not first, of course. No, first they all turned to look at Nathan. Then, they fell to her as if to survey what it took to have a man like that on your arm. She tried to suppress her smug look, but it felt pretty good to be the envy of everybody in there.

Nathan, of course, was oblivious to it. Sophie figured that he'd probably become desensitized to all the attention over the years. He just strode right up to the bar and ordered her drink for her.

She would have protested his dominance, except that he ordered exactly what she would have ordered herself. Pulling out a stool, Nathan gestured for her to sit. She perched on the chair opposite him, sipped her gin and tonic and marveled at the man who consistently kept surprising her. He was commanding without being overpowering and gentlemanly without being condescending. *What he is, is a sexy enigma. Why in the hell is he spending his time helping you?*

Since he'd shown up without warning at her door, neither of them had mentioned the kiss. She hadn't wanted to bring it up for fear of making things awkward. Not that she truly believed that Nathan would be remotely phased by it if she had.

It was more embarrassment on her part. The last thing she wanted was for him to think that she was making a big deal over something that was nothing to him. "So, before you start this bizarre tutorial of yours, why don't you tell me first why you were on that guest list of potential investors for my client's event?" She leaned forward, close to his face. "Who exactly are you, Nathan Windsor?"

It was the first time she'd noticed his confident and sturdy eye contact waver. It was so quick. If she hadn't been so close to him it would have been imperceptible, but the flicker of uncertainty had definitely been there.

Nathan sat back in his seat, a small frown marring his perfect face, and took a long drink before replying.

He sighed. "My family owns Windsor Corp. Up until a year ago, I was acting president."

"What happened a year ago?"

He studied her and swallowed. "I walked away from the company the night I met you at Thrive."

Sophie's mouth fell open and she flushed crimson red. "When did you finally remember?"

Nathan narrowed his gaze. "When did you remember?"

"The moment you moved in. But you didn't recognize me. So, no point bringing it up."

Nathan cursed under his breath. "I suppose there is no

point telling you I'm a wanker. In my defense though, your hair is different and you never wear it down."

Self-consciously, Sophie ran a hand through her hair. "Arsehole didn't like the red or my hair out."

"What? He's sexy intolerant or something? There are little blue pills for that now."

She blinked, then a laugh bubbled out. "Sexy intolerant?"

He grinned. "Yep."

"I was irritated you didn't remember."

His gaze met hers. "I wish I had remembered. Please tell me it wasn't that wanker you were waiting on."

She winced. "One and the same. I've been an idiot for a long damn time."

She needed to get his intense scrutiny off of her.

"Do you mind me asking what you and your dad fell out about then?"

He shook his head. "Let's just call it irreconcilable differences."

He'd hidden his notoriety quite well, she thought. Not the money so much. Being as rich as he was came with tells: the flat that cost more to rent in one month than most people earned in two years, the accent that dripped of private school, etc. That kind of infinite wealth was hard to disguise, and she didn't feel as though Nathan had tried to per say. But he was guarding something closer to his chest, and she was dying to know what it was.

≈

HE EXHALED, unable to quite believe that he was about to spill everything to this woman. In spite of himself, he found that he actually *wanted* to tell her everything. There'd never been much of an opportunity for him to offload to anyone before. Sophie made him feel so comfortable, like he could trust her. *Careful Nathan,* he warned himself.

"I don't really want to get too deep; we are supposed to be having fun here," he said. "But basically, my dad when I was growing up was a serial cheater. Swore he'd change, then would do it again. It killed my mum. Finally, she walked out. Just had enough, you know?"

"I can understand that."

"He was a complete twat to her. She died about six months after she left. Took a bunch of pills."

"Shit, Nathan. I'm so sorry."

He swallowed the well of emotion. If he didn't let himself feel, that shit couldn't hurt right? "Thanks. I was nine at the time and pretty messed up. But eventually things changed."

Nathan took a moment to sip some of his scotch. More than anything, he wanted to keep things lighthearted. He had built his walls and he liked them fine where they were. But Sophie was quiet. Patient. Kind. And out of nowhere he found himself talking.

"Dad met someone else—Judith. She practically brought me up. Judith didn't have kids of her own and she treated me like she would have done her own. She was, she is, my second mum and I love her like one. So ... almost a year ago, I found out that Dad's been shagging the head of marketing for over a year. Behind Judith's back." He shook his head. Even now, disbelief was his overriding feeling. "I just couldn't stomach looking at him anymore."

Sophie reached out and touched his arm. The gesture was nice, encouraging. "I walked out. Never went back."

"Does Judith know?" Sophie asked gently.

"No. I can't face her. I've told Dad that he needs to tell her. He's point-blank refused. Said the marketing bird was nothing. Meaningless. All the usual excuses. And he knows I'd rather die myself than hurt Judith. As far as I'm concerned, I want nothing more to do with him."

14

Shock. That was the only emotion that coursed through her veins. First at his honesty, then that he'd given her something so personal. And finally, how strongly he felt about his father's cheating. She'd taken him for a pussy hound, yes. She'd maybe subconsciously included thinking cheating was no problem.

Just another thing you were wrong about.

Had someone told her all this and then asked her opinion a week ago, she'd have quickly assumed that Nathan was a poor little rich boy who was quick to judge and only out for himself.

It seemed as though the more she learned about him, the more surprised she felt. He was certainly nothing like you'd assume he would be, if you were to judge purely on looks and snapshots of lifestyle.

"I'm sorry you've been through all that. Do you think that having an honest conversation with your dad might help? Why can't you explain it to him how you have to me?"

Nathan shook his head. "I don't want to have to. I want the man I used to admire to do the right thing and figure it out for himself." He shrugged, making his statement look more nonchalant than Sophie believed he really felt, and then he caught her eye.

His look sent a shiver of excitement through her. Despite having opened up to her about something so personal, the stormy depths of his eyes still contained that slightly mischievous light. If she stared too long, she knew for sure that her mind would wonder how that sexy mischief could manifest itself in the bedroom. She had to halt it before a blush crept over her cheeks and the inner workings of her mind would be visible to Nathan.

"Right. Now that I've told you my entire life history, I think it's time we get cracking." He glanced around the room. "You see anyone you like the look of?"

Sophie's heart sank. "We're really doing this, huh?" She had hoped ... It was stupid but she'd thought that they'd been connecting. She'd even been naive enough to hope that the whole training session was just a smooth ruse by him to get her on a date.

"Fuck yeah we're doing this."

Apparently not. "You need to find someone who you think looks fit, and then start a conversation. Once you've get to know them a bit, the most important thing is that you're honest and say that you're not after anything long-term."

I've found someone hot, Sophie looked at him, feeling

more disappointed than she really cared to admit. "And then what? How do I suddenly go from finding someone hot and taking him home to having no feelings for him the next day?"

"Because you control yourself. You know from the start it's a one night thing and so does he. It makes for a great, selfish fuck and you just kind of, hold back because you know it's just that night. Or afternoon. Whatever." He laughed at her skeptical impression. "I promise you it works. Only take numbers before you've had your fun and delete them afterward."

She twisted her fingers together, nervous and uncertain. She just wanted to stay right here, talking and drinking with Nathan. The way he'd kissed her had been so passionate, but then he said all that stuff about not becoming involved emotionally at all. He was such an infuriating paradox.

Feeling infuriated by him was such comfortable, familiar territory it spurred Sophie on to speak up. "Do you want another scotch? I mean, I appreciate you're taking time out to help me here, but I really think I'm gonna need a couple more drinks before I'm brave enough to approach some poor, unsuspecting dude."

Nathan held his hands up. "No pressure. Your call."

"Are you sure this is a good idea?"

Nathan gave her that lethal grin before he took a sip of his scotch. "Yes. Come on. you've got to do this. Just walk up to someone, smile, and be confident. I promise you: you're beautiful, so any guy you walk up to will preen. And then let him drive the conversation."

She scowled at him. "Yeah, you make that sound easy. Besides, aren't I supposed to let the guys chase me?"

He nodded. "Oh, you are. And you will. All you're doing is walking up and presenting the bait and saying hello. Let them do all the rest of the chasing. You're worth being chased."

Sophie was happy that at least he couldn't see her flush in this lighting. "Right. I'm worth the chase. All right then." She took her shot of tequila and poured it down the hatch. God, that burned. But she was going to need this mortification. "Okay, who were you pointing me at?"

Nathan surveyed the crowd at the bar. "The guy in a suit, no tie, in the corner by the door. He's been darting glances over here for a minute. He's trying to figure out if we're together or not."

Sophie slid a glance over. "Oh my God, he is ridiculously good-looking."

Nathan scoffed. "Please. You shagged hotter. Come on. Off you get."

Jesus Christ, how could he so casually talk about them having sex like that and feel absolutely nothing in terms of any jealousy? *This is how you need to be. No fear. No jealousy. Just go out there and lay it all out there.* "Okay, let's do this."

"Remember: walk up; smile; say hello. Let him do the work after that."

Right. He made it all sound so easy. But there was no backing out now. *Casual. Fun.* The whole point was to prove she could do this. *You're crazy.* Yes, yes she was, but she was doing it anyway.

It turned out that Nathan wasn't entirely wrong. The

moment she walked up to the suited guy by the door, he grinned. And when she said hi, he did take over. As it turned out, she didn't have to do much except stand there and smile, sip on her drink. It was easy, except he was dreadfully boring. He was a foot doctor or something. She hadn't really been paying attention. The whole time she could feel Nathan's gaze boring on her back. She wanted to turn to look at him. But that wasn't the point of this exercise. The point of this exercise was to meet someone. Someone like him, someone that she never even thought to try and get, someone exciting. That was not this guy.

So Doctor by the Door leaned forward. "What do you say we get out of here?"

Sophie blinked up at him. "Oh, out of here?" He was just asking to take her back to his place or something? Gosh, she was so out of practice with this. It turned out she needn't have panicked. She could feel the hand at the small of her back and she knew that touch. It was warm. Electrifying. It sent shivers up her back in the way that Doctor by the Door couldn't manage. What the hell was his name again?

"Excuse me, mate. I'm just going to go over here and sweep this beautiful girl for a moment."

Doctor by the Door scowled. "Just who the fuck do you think you are? Sophie and I were having a conversation."

Nathan didn't even skip a beat. "Oh, she didn't mention? She's already engaged, to me. We like to do this thing every once in a while where, you know, we invite someone else into our bed. I don't think I like the look of you. You don't look like you know how to suck—"

Doctor by the Door's eyes went wide and backed up a

step. Sophie whacked Nathan on the arm. "Oh my God, you are impossible."

He led her away. "He wasn't the right one for you anyway. Oh my God, I could actually see you falling asleep on your feet."

"But did you have to say that? Dear God, now he thinks—"

Nathan laughed. "Now he thinks you're extremely adventurous. Besides, it doesn't matter. It's not like you're going to go home with him anyway."

"Yeah, you have a point. God, he was boring."

But that didn't deter Nathan. He directed her toward an edgy looking guy at the end of the bar. "Okay, try him next."

Under this guy's rolled up sleeves, she could see hints of tattoos. He also had an earring in one ear. He was dressed sharp, but there was a hint of edge to him. "Oh, okay, that's more like it."

Nathan scowled. "You'd like him? I thought you had taste."

She laughed. "You're the one who said I need variety and fun. He looks like he might be fun. He's clearly not afraid of being a little bit edgy."

He nodded. "Yeah, whatever. Have at it. I'll be at the bar. Send up a smoke signal if you need it."

Turned out the guy at the end of the bar? His name was Adam. And surprise, surprise, he was a musician, which really didn't bother her much when she mentioned she was in promotions and events, he got extra chatty. Within five minutes of her conversation with him, he was closing out his tab and ready to go shag. Sure enough Nathan stepped in again.

This time, he pretended to be drunk. "Oh, sorry mate. Oh, I just tripped and couldn't get my bearings."

Adam scowled. "You need to watch where you're going mate. You got— fucking whatever that is all down my shirt."

Nathan shrugged. "I'm so sorry mate. Do you me to wipe it off?" He signaled the bartender. "Can I have a rag? I need to wipe down my man's back here."

Adam shook his head and excused himself to the bathroom.

When he was gone, Sophie turned to Nathan. "What was wrong with him? He was cute and fun."

Nathan shook his head. "Yes, good-looking, fun, but you were giving that face, like you might get attached to that one and that is not the point of this experiment. We want fun, good-looking and *disposable*."

"Yeah, but what's the problem if I get attached? He was very cute."

He shook his head. "Nope. Not that one. Pick another one."

And off it went for three more tries. Eventually all she got was frustration. After thirty more minutes, Nathan had found a way to essentially cock-block every single guy she walked up to. But, on the plus side, she was no longer nervous. And it was actually kind of fun.

"What about him?" Nathan asked.

Sophie shook her head. "No. No more guys because you're going to find something wrong with each and every one of them. I'm tired and I need to get my shoes off my feet."

He nodded. "You're right. These guys were dodgy anyway. We'll try again. Do you want to go and watch a movie? I'm in sort of an old action flick, martial arts kind of mood."

She blinked at him. "You want to keep hanging out? You know what? Actually that sounds kind of good. I'm exhausted. Getting hit on is hard."

He chuckled as he threw an arm around her. "See, that's what I've been trying to tell you this whole time."

The hours passed like lightning. Sophie enjoyed the way that she seemed to make Nathan laugh and she was much more relaxed around him than she thought she'd have been.

Not once was she aware that she sat drinking in a bar with one of the richest men in London, though she was constantly aware that she was sat drinking with one of the *hottest* men in England. Every time he looked at her she felt the flap of several hundred butterflies in her tummy and each woman that passed them looked on in awe. Some of them even had the audacity to smile or wave at him. Sophie was incredulous by this behavior; okay, so she wasn't on a date with him or anything, but it was still damn rude and disrespectful.

Nathan noticed but ignored them all. Unfortunately, his attention was completely on Sophie. It was unfortunate because she felt that if he could have at least lived up to her preconceptions of him being a womanizing philander who had no respect, it would have kept a bit of a lid on her ever increasing fantasies about him.

But she knew now that, even with extensive notches on his bedpost, he was extremely respectful. A womanizer he may have been, but he was no arsehole. In fact, Sophie was worried that he was quite the opposite.

NATHAN HAD WANTED Sophie to give it a go with someone that evening. She needed to get back on the horse. She didn't need any more tears shed over men that weren't worth it. But he could tell that she was still tense and not ready to try yet, and that was cool with him. He quite liked just hanging out.

He was getting closer to her than he would have liked; not that he normally kept secrets from the women he met, but he had never gone into quite so much detail before. She put him at ease and that, in turn, put him on edge.

Come on, you idiot. You've got friends you speak to; Sophie's just a new friend, that's all. But as he looked at her, he wondered if he really meant that.

After seeing how heartbreak had destroyed his father, he'd made a vow with himself never to be either the cause of it, or on the receiving end of it. And that meant not getting attached to the opposite sex, nor letting them get attached to him. He never wanted to experience that, not ever. He was, however, just a man. And she was a very pretty woman.

One simple kiss had gotten him all worked up last

night. And now he wanted to kiss her again. What the fuck was wrong with him? Dammit, he really wanted to see her naked. But honestly, he'd be perfectly happy sitting here talking to her all night. What the hell was wrong with him?

And as much inner turmoil as he was in, she seemed completely comfortable. He knew his effect on women. And he knew last night she'd wanted him. The problem was, while she was able to just file that away, *he* was still thinking about her.

For the first time, a woman had been able to walk away and he didn't entirely know what to do with that. It was new territory for him. Up until he'd met her, he would have been proud to tell anyone that he could read women like a book. Women were his area of expertise for God's sake. But not this one. He still couldn't figure her out.

It was difficult because he got on better with Sophie than he did some of his friends he'd known since childhood. He could say absolutely anything; nothing shocked or phased her. He could be unapologetically himself and not only did she accept it, she even teased him about some things too. The evening had been, unexpectedly, one of the best he'd had since arriving in London, and nobody had even taken their clothes off. *Yet.*

Fuck it. Go big or go home. Wasn't that what the Yanks said? He met her gaze with his. "Do you want to stay here and have another or do you fancy coming up to my much bigger flat?"

"You know, I am quite curious as to what the other side of the building looks like." She grinned. "I'll accept because I'm nosy."

The whole way home, all Nathan could think about was touching her. How had she gotten him so worked up? It was hardly as if she'd been laying the sexy attitude on thick; in fact, she'd been so casual with him she'd even snorted with laughter.

He was being pulled into her orbit despite it breaking all his rules, he actually wondered what it might be like to shag someone who he wanted to do more than just shag with. He was turned on by her personality. And that had never happened before.

You're in a twist mate.

Once inside the flat, she scoped it out by doing exactly as he had in hers, standing in the middle of the living room and surveying the area.

"This is insane," she said, looking around in marvel. "It feels like it's double the size of my place. How is that even possible?"

"Good interior designer." He shrugged, not confessing that he'd actually designed the interior himself. His creative side was a part of him he kept well hidden. Being a business man and an artist were two very conflicting roles. He liked keeping them separate. "Oh, and the fact that my flat is the bigger of our two." He smiled and nudged her affectionately. She retaliated immediately by shoving him hard with a laugh.

"So, what do you want to watch?"

Sophie frowned. "You were serious about the movie?"

"Of course. Did you think I invited you up here to have my way with you?"

~

Sophie flushed hot. Well, one could hope. But she hadn't been thinking that exactly. "No. I figured you'd ply me with alcohol and your bad taste in music first."

"You wound me. Pray tell me what is wrong with One Direction. I happen to think they have some soulful ballads. And that Harry, with the hair. He's very handsome." His lips twitched, giving him away.

"Let me guess: one of your female admirers loved them."

He nodded. "You guessed it. In retrospect, I should never have given her a repeat showing. Except she did this thing with her tongue—" He cut himself off.

Sophie leaned closer. "Oh, c'mon. You have to tell me now. You cut my lesson off downstairs. I want to know what skill I can learn with my tongue to warrant a repeat performance."

He cleared his throat and slid his gaze away. "We'll move on to the bedroom skill later. Have a seat. Can I get you anything?"

"Wine is good. I'm not picky."

He came back from the kitchen with two glasses of something white and chilled. While he'd been gone, she couldn't help a little light snooping. There were photos of him looking younger with a woman smiling. Many with him and friends. None with anyone that might look like his father.

There was a larger one near the window. He was clearly younger. Maybe eight? With a beautiful woman. He got his blue eyes and mischievous smile from her. Sophie's heart went out to him. The pain he must have gone through.

"Here you are. So what do you want to watch?"

She joined him on the couch as he pulled up the digital movie shelf on the telly screen.

"What do you have?"

"Everything. Honestly, Mum loved movies and theater. She used to take me to all those shows in the West End. I got bitten by the same bug. Let me guess. You want something sappy? I have *Love Story.*"

She set her glass on the coffee table next to his. "Hello, jilted woman here. What about me makes you think I want to watch a love story?"

He chuckled. "Sorry?"

"I mean the only way I want to watch a love story is if it's got a naked Jamie Dornan in it."

"You think that's a love story? I swear to God, women have no idea what they want."

She playfully shoved his shoulder. "Hell yeah. At the very least if I'm going to have to endure two people falling in love, let me get some good sex out of it. It's been too long."

In that moment, she wanted to recall the words. The last thing she needed to think about was sex when she was around him. *But it's too late for that now, isn't it?*

THE ATMOSPHERE CRACKLED AROUND THEM. Her hands on him were a challenge and her words were a taunt. No way in hell he was going to survive that movie with her so close. Things were bad enough. For once he was trying to be a gentleman. "Your ex should be shot, do you know that?"

"Oh yeah. I know it."

"Just how long *has* it been?" Stupid. Stupid. Stupid. *Why ask her that unless you want to picture shagging her seven ways from Sunday?*

When she met his gaze, the atmosphere changed in a blink. Her pupils dilated and her lips parted. He knew she wanted him. He could almost taste her.

Nathan's cock turned to steel from one glance. There had been a twenty-four hour build up to this moment, and he was determined to make the most of it.

"I'm going to kiss you now," he said, sliding his hands around her waist. She didn't reply, just nodded her head once. Slowly. *Yes.*

He cupped her cheek in his hand and hovered, his lips just millimeters from hers. As he watched the way her bottom lip quivered at the anticipation, his blood thickened with an injection of lust. His dick ached and he welcomed the feeling. Reveled in the anticipation. She was his. *For tonight.* Yeah, of course, that's what he meant.

The throbbing in his jeans became more of a surge when their lips touched. She tasted sweet. Soft. He teased his tongue over her bottom lip until she gasped and parted for him, his tongue easing inside her mouth.

She was even softer inside. And sweet. So sweet. Her tongue met his briefly, in a slow slick freefall.

It was intimate and sensual. "I've been waiting a long time to touch you," Nathan breathed, standing back slightly and unbuttoning the front of her dress. He loved buttons. They were the reason he'd suggested she wear this outfit earlier when she'd asked him to pick something for her.

Buttons revealed the gift underneath much slower than a zip. Bit by bit, Nathan uncovered the edge of her black bra. He could see the swell of her breast above it, a swollen semi-circle half encased in lace.

Bending down, he kissed along the swell, using one hand to continue with the buttons, unwrapping her slowly, and the other to squeeze the underside of her breast. With the edge of his thumb, he flicked her hardening nipple beneath the silky fabric.

One hand smoothing over her waist, he deepened their kiss. Taking long drugging pulls at her lips and eliciting a moan out of her.

So damn perfect. He felt like someone had hooked his body up to a defibrillator, the kiss was so charged. Their only points of contact were her hands on his waist, his hand in her hair and on her hip, and their lips. But it was enough to send his heart into a gallop and for the blood to rush in his ears.

The kiss shook him. He'd kissed a lot of women. Certainly, more than his fair share. But with Sophie, his body hummed and his synapses shorted. Tugging her closer, he licked into her mouth. Sophie moaned and slid her arms up to wind around his neck.

"You are so fucking sexy. Your boyfriend was blind."

Once he'd slowly unbuttoned her to the navel, he slipped her dress down her hips and onto the floor. Then his gaze flickered to hers.

Her pupils were now so dilated that even the green flecks had vanished, giving way to a dark charcoal.

He wrapped his arms around her back, gently unhooking her bra. "I keep obsessing about your taste." He couldn't help groaning as he finally got to place Sophie's nipple in his mouth. Flicking it hard with his tongue, he felt her tense up with a soft gasp. As he used his teeth to nibble on her, she moved her hands across his shoulders, pulling at his shirt.

He took the hint, pulling himself upright and taking off his T-shirt. Sophie whimpered and then reached out, running her fingers down his torso. His cock twitched with desire as she traveled further down toward the waistband of his jeans.

The low moan that came from her throat sounded like a purr, rolling over him like a caress. Nathan picked her up easily and repositioned them on the couch. He managed to wrangle his shirt off, and then shucked his jeans, leaving him in just his boxers with her in her knickers and bra.

Pulling her toward him, their mouths met with a clash. Fuck, he couldn't take the teasing.

"Fuck, Sophie, how wet are you? Do you want me as much as I want you?" he murmured against her lips.

From her position straddling him on the couch, she rocked over the length of him and he cursed low.

"I want to see how wet you are. I want to feel my cock against your pussy lips." His dick straine against his boxers, raging hard. Sophie's eyes fell right to it, followed by her hands. Tantalizingly, she used the edge of her finger-nail to graze a trail around his wanting dick, circling the length and then moving down to his balls. Her breathing was heavy in his ear.

Her hot, slick center slid over the cotton-clad length of him and his eyes crossed. Damn. He fought for control, fought to stay steady. He didn't want to go too fast. To ruin this.

"Nathan," she moaned, her breathing harsh and labored and her back bowed beneath him. He ran his nose along her skin to the hollow of her throat.

"I've been dying to kiss you here, too." He blew a breath over her heated flesh down to one raised breast. Sliding his hands up her torso, he took his time, running his fingers over her ribs and her soft skin. When he palmed her, she moaned, arching into the caress.

Her hips lifted again and again, starting them on a rhythm that wouldn't stop. Placing kisses all along her chest, Nathan teased her nipple with his thumb and tested the weight of her breast, making the both of them crazy. Every time his mouth went near the peaked tip, she writhed on top of him.

Sliding a hand between them, he tucked his curious fingers into her knickers and stroked her soft, slick flesh. "You're wet," he muttered, loving that liquid was already ready for him. "Do you even understand what you've been doing to me?" he asked through clenched teeth. "Do you know how many nights I've gone to bed thinking about how you'd taste? I feel like I need to show you the fantasies. Every single one."

She tensed for a moment then shivered as he stroked her slit again.

"Yes," she whispered. "Please."

He finally took the stiff peak in his mouth. She drew in a shuddering breath, and he growled his satisfaction as his hand busied himself with her other breast. Sucking, licking and teasing with his tongue and his teeth, he took her to the edge and back again.

Nathan grazed her nipple with his teeth as his finger found her wet and inviting. Slowly, he dipped inside her sex, testing her, seeing how ready she was—how much she wanted him. He was in no hurry and could do this all night.

He released her breast and she whimpered, trying to bring him back. But instead, he kissed his way back up her body. Taking her lips again, he timed his finger with the deep strokes of his tongue.

Against his thigh, his erection throbbed and begged for relief, but this was about her—about seeing her fly. He could wait. Gritting his teeth against the need, he dragged his lips from hers, trailing them along her jawline to her neck, and she shivered.

Her hands traced up his back, her nails digging into his bunched and flexed muscles. "Nathan, please hurry. I need —" Before she could finish, her slick, slippery flesh quivered around his fingers.

He pulled back to watch her wide-eyed, blissed-out expression. Seeing her lashes flutter closed and her mouth parted on a silent scream of ecstasy, he demanded, "Look at me, Sophie. I want you to look at me while you come. Who is making you feel like this?"

She opened her eyes and met his gaze with a shocked

expression as her body tightened around his exploring fingers again. His thumb ghosted over her pleasure button, and his name was a moan on her lips as she came again.

"Oh God, Nathan. You are."

"Good. We're off to a good start." Nathan gentled his strokes, but he didn't stop. He wasn't done with her yet. He wanted her boneless by the time they were done. Then he wanted to start all over again. With each gentle glide, he nuzzled at her neck, sipped at her lips, nipped at the flesh of her collarbone. "Now do you remember that night a year ago? Do you remember what I was doing to the blonde with my fingers?"

She stilled. "N—Nathan?"

"Easy does it. I'm just going to tease a little. We'll have plenty of time for that. Do you trust me, Sophie?" Even as he asked the question, he used his free hand on her arse to guide her motions over his still-cotton-clad dick. "Did you think about it? Maybe when you were alone with your toys, did you think about me?"

His fingers gently slid over the pucker of her arse, and she shivered. "Oh my God, that feels—"

He did it again, effectively cutting off any thought. "Forbidden, dirty, sexy?"

"Yes, all of it. God, I just want you."

Gently, he teased her even as his thumb continued to slide over her clit. How had he ever thought her uptight? In his arms, she was melting chocolate, rich and decedent. "Nathan, please. I need you. I just—" Her legs clamped around his hips and she broke apart again in his arms.

He grinned to himself as he gently pulled his fingers

from her. When she sagged against his shoulder, he shifted them until she lay back on the couch and he reached for his wallet, pulling out a condom. In seconds, he was kicking aside his boxers and had himself sheathed.

When he crawled up over her, she reached for him. A shiver ran through him, and he bit his lip. When he lined his erection up with her sweet center and slid home, they both gasped, the breath rushing out of their lungs.

"Fuck, you're tight. So goddamned tight," he muttered to himself. *Jesus. Go slow. Go slow. Do not rush this.* But it didn't take long before the need was tingling and spiraling along his spine. She stroked his back and met him thrust for thrust, holding eye contact.

Shit. For the first time, he felt like someone was looking clear into his soul. The emotions were too raw, too hard to confront, so he tucked his head into her neck. "You remember that dirty little thing I introduced to you just now? Let me show you how fun it can be." He tucked his hands under her arse and dragged her closer.

As he dipped his head to take a pert nipple into his mouth, his middle finger found her arsehole and he gently pushed against it. Sophie threw her head back, his name on her lips in a scream.

He timed the thrusting of his dick with his finger and sucked her nipple deep. This time when her inner walls fisted around his cock, there was no holding back. She pulsed around him, milking his cock, and he finally let the reins of control go. With one more stroke, he dove headfirst off the cliff, coming so hard he was sure he was never going to remember his name again.

15

Yet another night passed where Nathan was the cause for Sophie not being able to sleep. Back in her own flat, she lay in bed in the dead of night replaying the sex and not being able to stop herself from smiling.

She remembered the look in his eyes, the hunger he seemed to have for her.

When he'd laid her back on the sofa, she'd been grinning from ear to ear. From where she was lying, she had a view of his entire body: his broad, tanned shoulders, solid pectoral muscles and deliciously prominent abs forming a gloriously symmetrical eight-pack. She hadn't even believed eight-packs had really existed before, thinking that they were some sort of myth. It wasn't any wonder that she had been smiling really.

And his dick ... *Oh my god.*

He'd bent his knees so that his cock was level with the entrance to her pussy and just looked at her.

Taking himself into his hand, he'd rubbed the head of

his dick up and down, making her wetter. When he reached her clit, he stopped momentarily, pressing firmly against it. The hardness of him made her pussy throb so deep inside that her breath caught.

"Fuck, you feel incredible. So wet," he'd growled, dipping just his tip into her entrance and then sliding it back out with excruciating slowness.

At one point he'd said, "I want you to look at me. I want to watch your face as I push my dick in and out of your wet pussy." Like holy shit. The talking dirty thing was so … bloody, fucking fantastic. She never thought she'd like it, but with Nathan? Hell yes.

He'd asked her things like, "Do you want me to touch your clit?"

The answer was always, *Bloody hell, yes*. She'd had to bite her lip and nod at that point. There was no way that she'd have been able to form any coherent words. His fingers trailed across her navel and down to her bud. He teased it, watching it swell and stiffen at his touch.

Sophie's eyes rolled in the back of her head. Good lord, was it possible to die from orgasm?

He'd had to hold her for quite some time afterward. Every time he moved even the slightest bit, she shook so badly she thought she might pass out. It was as though he had stripped back every nerve, leaving them all exposed and raw.

When she eventually did stop shaking, she felt as though her bones had turned to water. She was completely limp and unable to move, and she burst into peals of laughter.

"Jesus, that was incredible," she breathed.

Nathan's smile had been wide and cocky. "I aim to please."

She had watched him quietly as his eyes shuttered. She'd seen in his eyes that he'd felt it too.

Sophie had left as soon as she felt able to stand up without fainting. He'd been very clear that his other, erm, *companions,* never stuck around, and she didn't want him to have to ask her to leave. Above anything else, she was afraid that him asking her to go would hurt her and ruin this incredible high. It was better that she took it upon herself.

Had she been played? Had he just been trying to prove a point with her? That he could have her?

No, that couldn't be what it was, surely? The sex they'd had, it had been too good, he'd been too sincere … She stopped, her good mood now painted in black.

She was already attached. Of course she was; she'd been the one being played, not the other way round—as had been the initial plan for her evening. She'd been attached from the moment that he'd stood up for her with Christopher.

And now she realized that she was just another one of his many, many women and that she'd probably never hear from him again.

16

She'd left him. Nathan pondered that as he stretched along his couch. All he knew was sometime in the middle of the night when he'd reached for her, she wasn't there. They'd had, what? Three rounds? When he'd woken, it wasn't even light out.

But now that he was awake and alert, he knew for sure she was gone. And the telly was off. Hell, she'd even fully covered him with a blanket. Fuck *me*.

What the fuck had happened? Sometime between finding out she was the redhead from last year and trying to teach her to be casual she'd blown his mind. And somehow, he felt decidedly *not* casual about shagging her.

Talk about a first.

Usually he was the one sneaking out in the middle of the night under the cover of darkness. What the hell was that hollow feeling in the center of his chest? He didn't enjoy that one bit. She'd had fun right? And they were friends? Well *now*, they were friends. He wasn't a random hookup. *Or are you?*

Why did it even matter?

Oh, it mattered. He liked her. And now that he knew who she was he wanted to find out what made her tick. That charge of electricity between them from the night they'd first met, *what* the hell was that? *Why* the hell was that?

Why couldn't he shake her?

You need to figure out how to do just that.

"Fuck! I'm so fucked." He scrubbed a hand over his stubble.

He didn't even like her. Well, he did. She was cool, and he could talk to her. And she wasn't crazy, which these days was a feat in and of itself. Why the fuck had she left?

Isn't that what you were teaching her? Well yes. But she wasn't supposed to do that to him. That shit was different.

Did she regret it? It had been clear what was going to happen the moment he kissed her. She hadn't stopped. She hadn't run away, so why leave in the middle of the night?

Maybe because she knows you. You're a manwhore.

That was likely an explanation, but still though, he hated that she'd left. He didn't want to think about the reasons why he hated it. Nathan pushed himself into a sitting position and scrubbed a hand over his face. This all could have a far simpler reason. Maybe she had to work. But he didn't know.

Or you could just ask her. Oh yeah, I'd come across like a needy git. That was probably something that Teabag Christopher would do.

And on that topic, how had she gone out with that guy for so long? At the same time, maybe if he just talked to her, things would be easier. He could assure her that last night hadn't meant anything.

It was just thorough sex. Making her feel good, taking her mind off of everything. And he liked her genuinely as a person. She wasn't all fucked in the head like he was.

Yeah, that's what he would do, talk to her. How hard could that be?

Also, why is it so important to you?

He shoved that thought aside. They'd agreed to be friends. *And then you slept with her.* Yes, but that was a friendly shag. It didn't mean anything. *Liar.*

No. He could do that. He'd show her that they could be friends. That no emotions needed to get untangled. He'd take her some coffee, they'd talk it out, and maybe this time, he wouldn't think with his dick.

Yeah, sure you won't.

17

The banging on the door woke Sophie out of her stupor. God, she was exhausted. And her limbs were far too languid for her liking. Not to mention she was .... sore in places but a good kind of sore.

A *well shagged* sore. God, when was the last time she felt like this?

She dragged herself out of bed, and grabbed her robe on the way. She squinted when she passed the mirror. Perhaps a breath mint wouldn't be the worst idea in the world. She grabbed one of the breath strips from her vanity and popped it in her mouth. She might look like hell, but at least she wouldn't have the worst morning breath.

She padded barefoot into her living room and then jogged to the door when the pounding on the door didn't let up. "Hold your horses. I'm coming. Jesus." When she dragged the door open, her breath caught. It wasn't a delivery.

Rather it was ... of the Nathan variety. He was leaning

against her doorjamb, a couple of coffees in hand, and what looked like they might be pastries from the bakery around the corner.

"You woke up before I could feed you breakfast. So, this will have to do. You missed out on my world-famous breakfast and a shag. So, you know, I make a mean eggs Benedict and then I do this thing with my fingers while you eat … " His voice trailed off. "Never mind all that."

Sophie stared at him and she could feel the flush crawling up her chest, and then her neck, and then inflaming her face. "Nathan—I, uh, didn't expect to see you."

His gaze was impassive. "Well, are you going to let me in? Coffee is getting cold." He brushed past her into her living room and headed straight to the dining table.

"How did you know I drink coffee?"

He set the drinks and the pastries down. "I paid attention. I see you on those mornings that you're carrying your drinks up the stairs to your flat. And I always see it's coffee. Besides, most people make tea at home and on their own."

Fuck, what the hell was she supposed to say?

"Uhh, excellent deductive reasoning."

He shrugged. "I do pay attention."

That he did.

Flashes of what they'd done last night crept into her brain, making her warm, soften and throb in places. He *had* paid attention. *Close attention.* When she liked something, he did it again, and again, until it drove her so crazy she screamed. When she clearly wasn't as into something, he'd moved on instead of trying to impose what he wanted to do.

He'd been the perfect lover. But of course, he knew that. But now was not the time to think about that. Now was the time to figure out what he was doing in her flat and send him packing. She hadn't wanted an awkward morning after. Except it didn't seem like he was awkward at all. And he'd brought her coffee and pastries.

"What's up, Nathan? I, uh, didn't think I'd see you."

He picked up one of the coffees out of the tray and walked over to give it to her before shoving his hands into his jeans. "Well, you left. I figured it must have been some kind of emergency so I wanted to check on you."

Way to make her feel bad.

"No, uh, no emergency. I just woke up and I figured you know, you wouldn't be too keen on me being in your flat when you woke up."

His gaze narrowed. "Are you sure that's what you thought?"

"Uh what do you mean?" she said, hesitating.

No. That wasn't what she thought. She'd gone running for the hills because last night was supposed to be about casual sex. Having fun. It was supposed to be flirty and inconsequential. Except it made her feel … *things*. Well, not just those things, but *other* things. *Emotional* things. She had never had casual sex before, but she was pretty sure getting the emotional tinglies was not supposed to happen.

He studied her closely before nodding. "Okay, I get this is new to you. We're friends now, so I'll fill you in on how this goes."

She lifted a brow. "Oh, Sexual Yoda, explain it to me."

"You and I are sort of friends now. The way it works is we don't sneak out. It sucks."

She bit the inside of her cheek. "Never happened to you before huh?"

He shook his head.

She frowned. The tight set of his lips warned her that something was off. He'd wanted her to stay? "I'm sorry. I didn't think anything of it."

"Yeah, okay. Cheers. Listen, so I had an idea."

Sophie shook her head. "Oh man, I feel like I should be concerned."

He shook his head before grabbing his own coffee from the to-go tray. "No, I'm just saying, like you said last night. You haven't had the best of luck with boyfriends."

She flushed again. God, what was wrong with her? Why the hell couldn't she shut up around this guy? Instead, here she was spilling all of her secrets. "Yeah, I was sort of hoping that you could just forget all of that deep sharing stuff."

He chuckled but shook his head. "No, I don't get to forget that I shared my secret passion for entertainment. You don't get to shy away from this."

SHE SWALLOWED HARD AND NODDED. "Fair enough. So, what's your proposal?""Well, you're not shagging anyone at the moment, and you were saying that you've never had fun, never had adventure sex."

She couldn't hide the small smirk even as heat flamed

her face. "Well, now I can say I have." When she met his gaze again, he was grinning like an idiot.

"Yeah, well that's just my point. I've got plenty of adventure sex under my belt." She scrunched her nose. He muttered a curse. "That's not what I meant. Bugger, this isn't usually that hard." He shook his head. "What I meant to say is I can give you a no strings fun scenario. *And* I happen to be interesting and fun in and out of bed. And you don't seem to know that you deserve a lot better than that guy, so maybe you let me show you."

Sophie frowned. "What? Friends who shag?"

"Yeah."

"We barely know each other."

"Hear me out. I'm not sleeping with anyone steady at this time. I'll still give you coaching and dating lessons, but we just have a no strings sex situation. And if you find someone who you want to bone, just tell me and we're done. No harm. No foul."

Sophie blinked. And then she blinked again. What the hell? "So, you want us to *keep* sleeping together?"

His frown was slight. "Purely for fun of course. The moment you find a new boyfriend, we stop. It's more experimental. For me, you're beautiful, and I know you're not actually interested in me so I don't have to worry about you trying to cling. And for you, for once, you get some fun. And then with everything I show you, you can finally figure out what you'd like. And you can find the right kind of guy to show that to you." She still couldn't believe what she was hearing. "So, you want to sleep with me?" He laughed. "Well, I am a bloke, and you're worth it. So, default answer is always yes, but more than that, I like you and I think it's a bloody shame what you've been settling for."

"I—I don't even know what to say."

"Think of it as cutting your teeth on me."

She frowned. "You want me to bite you?"

He grinned. "You can if you want. It'll at least let me know you're having a good time, but uh, only in nonsensitive areas."

Sophie snorted. "You know what I meant by that."

His eyes widened and he raised his brows. "Moi? Do I?"

"I swear to God, you're incorrigible. You know you do."

"Let me stop joking make it clear," he said as he stepped forward, placed his coffee on the coffee table and stepped into her space, crowding her. His scent enveloped her, making her forget things like her name, where she was, and just who he was. For a fleeting moment, she wanted to believe that he could want her.

"What I'm saying, Sophie, is that I had fun. And that thing you did with your tongue was near life changing. I'd frankly like to keep shagging you. And I'll let you know before I start messing about with someone else. One thing though: when we're fucking, there should be no sneaking out. There'll be times when I want you and if I have to hunt you down and get it, that'll annoy me. And when I'm annoyed, I tend to want to take it out by licking you." He pulled her close and nuzzled her neck. "So, what do you say, Sophie?"

Was it her, or had his stormy blue eyes gone darker?

Was his voice deeper? She licked her lips. "I didn't mean to sneak off."

He shook his head. "It's fine. We're just friends who shag. But I woke up, wanting to hear you make that sound again and you were gone. I was miffed."

"Well, I don't know exactly how to do this. I figured, once you woke up you'd realize, 'well, I've shagged her now, I can stop pretending to like her.' "

He shook his head. "You don't know me that well. We should fix that. What do you say, Sophie? Do you want to be my very special friend?"

"Why do I get the feeling I'm getting more out of this than you are?"

He shook his head and licked his lips and Sophie's core contracted. "Then I guess I'll have to be more forthcoming. I think I can manage that."

She shook her head. "You're serious?"

He nodded. "Let me show you how much."

Sophie couldn't help but laugh and cover her face. "Why do I have the feeling that I'm going to get into a lot of trouble with you?"

He grinned. "That's because you are."

18

"So, what? You guys are two mates who spend a lot of time together naked?"

Sophie giggled when she thought about just how much they'd seen each other naked.

"I guess so. I mean I didn't go into any of this intending to shag him. It just sort of happened. We were there in his flat watching a movie and then he's kissing me and Jesus Christ, the man should give bloody lessons. I felt like slapping every bloke I've ever been with and saying, 'This is the example of how to kiss a woman, amongst other things.'"

Gemma hooted. "Oh my God, I'm going to need a full blow by blow. Dirty pun intended. Right now, I had to go get samples for the MacArthur wedding. I'm glad we got to have lunch though."

"Me too."

"Listen though, love. Be careful with this. You don't want to catch a case of feelings."

Sophie stood and gave her a hug. "Thanks for listening.

And thanks for not calling me insane. And I promise I'm not going to break the rules and develop feelings."

Gemma shook her head as she squeezed her tight. "Look, whatever makes you happy. You deserve better than Christopher. And right now, this bloke is offering you hot sex and fun with no strings attached. Where do I get that deal? And from the look on your face, you like it. So, have fun."

"You know what, Gemma? You're actually very smart."

Her friend grinned. And with a light dancing in her green eyes, she said, "Okay, let me go. But call me later and tell me everything. Especially about the next time you shag."

Sophie laughed. "Yeah, you got it."

After Sophie took care of the bill, she grabbed her purse and was headed back toward her flat when she heard her name called.

"Sophie."

She'd know that voice anywhere. Mostly because she'd heard it over and over in her head, she knew that timbre well. It was the same timbre Nathan used as he whispered her name in her ear when he was inside her. Slowly driving her insane, making her mad, making her want to come.

She whipped around. "Nathan, what are you doing here?"

"I am actually off to check out a new client. There's a technology show around the corner. I want to kind of go incognito, see how these things work without the benefit of lots of R and D guys behind the scenes making it work for a demo. Hence the baseball hat. I feel like it makes me look like a Yank."

She laughed. "You are definitely incognito. I didn't recognize you for a second." The casual look suited him. Ripped jeans, trainers, a plain white T-shirt that pulled tight across his chest and hugged the shoulders quite nicely, and a baseball hat. He could be some anonymous tourist. A very sexy anonymous tourist. Her whole body ached. "You want to come with me?"

"What? Right now?"

He nodded. "Yeah, why not?"

"I can't. I have a work thing. But I'm headed that way, if you want to walk together."

He nodded. And as they walked, Sophie wasn't sure what to do. She could feel the tension between them. It was almost as if their arrangement only worked well in darkness. As if neither one of them knew what to do with the other. "This is weird, isn't it?"

Sophie laughed. "Yes, very weird considering we weren't really even friends until, well, you know."

"Look. Come on; I'll walk you through the tube." He put an arm around her shoulders, and Sophie couldn't help but sink into the embrace. His warmth, his strength. God, the way he smelled was divine. When they rounded the corner, they glanced up at the Timmons Theater. The place had been there for decades, managing to withstand the new theaters opening in the West End.

Sophie frowned. "Oh, they're doing *Pygmalion*. I love *Pygmalion*."

"My mother *loved* that play."

Sophie frowned up at the sign. "Oh no, that's so sad. The theater is closing. I remember I came here with my school once."

He frowned. "This was like an institution in this neighborhood. I wonder why it's closing."

She slid her glance over to him. "Well, you did say that you wanted to do something different. Considering how much you love movies and theater (and how much your mother loved it), if the theater is closing, maybe you could do something about it."

His gaze met hers and held for a moment as they stood on the corner right outside the tube station, and then he lifted his eyes, looking back up at the theater. "You know what? Maybe you're right. Maybe I could do something about it."

19

Nathan watched Sophie as she skipped down the stairs of the tube. He couldn't shake the feeling. He liked her a lot and being around her felt good. He was supposed to be teaching her to have fun. *And kissing is part of this?* Yeah, okay it sounded like a bad idea. But really, what could go wrong?

It's perfectly normal. She was beautiful. When he kissed her, they were pretty much molten lava. But it was more than that. She made him laugh. And, she had this "dive headfirst into adventure" way about her. Even if she was scared, she'd still do it. He had to respect that. What he didn't like was her taste in guys.

When he'd suggested she get a little practice with the opposite sex, he hadn't realized quite how successful they would be. Even with her fake sense of bravado, that confidence had come across as sexy. It made every single man she walked up to interested in her, curious, willing to find out more. That irked him. Why?

Fuck him. Maybe they should stop. He waited for the claustrophobic feeling he got when he wanted to run. But it wasn't there. Maybe he was worried about nothing. It wasn't like he wanted her for himself. He was just being protective.

Yeah, whatever you need to tell yourself.

After he was sure she was safely down the stairs of the tube, he turned back around to stare at the theater. Yes, while there were many theaters in London that would show *Pygmalion* again, he didn't like the idea that *this* theater, one his mother had brought him to, was closing down. *Well, if you don't like it, do something about it.* Sophie's words kept clinging in his head. *You're in a position to do something, so do something.* She was right. Maybe it was finally time to do something that he wanted to do instead of what was expected.

His mind still full of thoughts of Sophie, he crossed the street and stopped in front of the Timmons Theater. For some reason, there was something holding him back. Something that kept him from barging in the way he normally would have. He had zero idea what to do in this scenario and it terrified the hell out of him.

Maybe fear is a good thing.

When it came to business, there was a reason that his father counted on him. There was a reason that old man had been hounding him to come back. There was a reason his stepmother had called and begged on behalf of his father. He was good at what he did. He knew the playing field. He knew the players. He understood the rules. This, this would be different. Uncharted territory. He would have to learn and learn quickly. And there would be mistakes made.

Find out the rules and beat them at their own game. Or, you could go back to what you know. No. He need to make a definitive break.

Nathan stared up at the signage that had once been so exciting to him as a kid. And then he made this decision. It was now or never.

It was time to take a risk.

∾

"Hello, this is Sophie."

"Sophie, this is Maria Delgado from Let the Girls Run. I was given your name from a Becca Dawston. She said you did a fantastic job for their charity event."

Sophie had to think back. Dawston. Dawston? Oh, yeah, they'd done a massive fund-raiser for a number of charities around London, all of which supported school-age girls and their quest to strengthen themselves. "Yes, I remember her. We had a great time with that. What is it I can help you with?"

"She said you did a fantastic job. In all honesty, I need to tell you that our budget is significantly smaller than theirs. We're a very small shop. We don't have much money, but we could definitely use the fund-raising help. And the events that you set up for the girls are something we're definitely looking forward to. Would you have some time to be able to chat about it?"

Sophie held her breath. Limited budget meant bare

bones. *But again, this is exactly what you said you wanted to do.* It was. She could actually be doing some good instead of just spoiling the needy. She could make a difference.

"Don't worry about your budget. Just tell me what it is you need and we can work it out."

"Oh my gosh, that's brilliant. I was worried to call you actually. I know that you work for Glass Slipper Events. But I was hoping that you'd contract this as well."

"Yes, I do. But I'm actually open for a pro bono work. So all you have to do is let me know what you need. When do you want to meet up?"

"Oh, thank God. I'm free this afternoon if you are."

As she got the details of what was needed, she couldn't believe her luck. She was finally getting to do something that she'd been talking about for so long. And most importantly, it felt awesome. She could still do her job and do this.

When she hung up, she did a little dance and picked up her phone. Oddly, the first person she wanted to call wasn't the number one on the speed dial. Number one was Gemma. But the person she wanted to call was Nathan.

Why was it she wanted to call him instead of Gemma? Gemma was her best school friend. The two of them were thick as thieves.

You know why. That unsettled her more than anything else. The rules with Nathan were clear. She was not to fall for him. He was just fun. He was an easy way to pass some time. And she was learning things. That was all.

Oh yeah? Then why is he the first one you want to call to tell you about your good news?

Never mind that. Instead of calling him, she very deliberately went to speed dial number one and dialed Gemma. Gemma would be thrilled to hear her news. She didn't need to tell Nathan anything. *Yeah, just keep telling yourself that.*

20

He should never have answered the call. Nathan knew it the moment he'd seen the somewhat familiar number. But he had, which was why he just spent the last three hours dealing with a client call for his father. A client, previously his, who couldn't get a hold of the old man. And of course, when they didn't call the old man to talk to him about it, it hadn't gone well.

"I don't understand why you don't just come back. You think you're better at my job than I am?"

"Dad, I left for a reason. And would you stop with the antics? Having clients calling me? It's not going to end well. You're going to lose them and I won't be able to do anything about it."

"Is that a threat?"

And it just deteriorated from there. By the time he reached the bar where he was meeting Garrett, he was exhausted, cranky, and in no mood.

"Mate, you look like you could use a drink."

"Yeah, I *feel* like I could use one too."

Garrett chuckled. "Let me guess: the old man?"

Nathan shook his head. "It's like he's deliberately sabotaging the whole company just to force my hand to come back. I'm not going back."

His friend only chuckled and took a sip of his Guinness. "Are you sure about that? You left what? Nine months ago? I know that you have a few of your own clients, the start-up type stuff, but honestly, like it or not, Windsor Corp. is still the two ton behemoth in the game. And you were very good at your job. Your portfolio reflects that."

Garrett, as his accountant, kept an eye on his bottom line. The two of them had been friends since St Andrews.

"It's not about the bottom line, Garrett. It's about him taking the bloody piss. Oh, by the way, I should probably tell you. I bought a theater."

Garrett stopped mid sip of his beer, "Excuse me?"

Nathan nodded. "The Timmons Theater. I saw that it was being closed down, so I bought it."

His friend stared. "Aren't you supposed to discuss major purchases with me?"

"I won't even notice the loss of funds. Besides, it's for a good cause. The theater owners can get back on their feet with a little direction from me."

Garrett shook his head. "Seriously, what's gotten into you?"

"Nothing, I'm fine. So yeah." He shrugged. "I bought a theater."

Garrett just tossed his arms up. "Fine, you bought a theater. Make sure to send me some specifics in the morning. I'll look at the contract, get everything signed, etc. But please no more theater buying. At least give me a call, or text me something so I can draft the contract properly."

Nathan shrugged. "Fair enough, but I don't know. I saw it today when I was walking in the West End. And I just —"

Garrett chuckled again. "You were just walking around, just taking the day off to stroll around London?"

Nathan shrugged. "I guess."

"I don't think I've ever known you to do that."

What the hell was he getting at?

"Well, there's a first time for everything."

It didn't matter what Garrett said or did. His mood was still shit. Nathan tried to get into the spirit and he and Garrett hadn't caught up in over a month. But he couldn't help it. He wasn't just in the mood.

A sexy blonde passed by them a couple of times. Each time she made eye contact with him. Oh boy, he knew what was coming. Eventually she just walked over, looking the two of them directly in the eye. "Hi, I'm Ivy." And then she waited for one of them to say something.

Garrett, understanding his role in all this, took the lead and immediately started talking to her. But she was looking at Nathan. As they chatted, she found excuses to brush her hand along his knee or his arm. Nathan knew this dance. He had perfected this dance. And honestly, a good, long shag would do wonders to improve his mood.

Only problem was, he really wasn't into it. Oh sure, she was fit. Long, toned legs. Great smile. But somehow the last thing he wanted to do was toss her around the bed.

Garrett gave him a lifted brow as if to ask, "What the hell is wrong with you?"

The blonde started chatting with the girl near their booth for a moment and as he watched her, Nathan had a feeling he knew what was wrong with him, but he didn't feel like dealing with that right now. "Mate." He leaned forward so Garrett could hear him. "I think I want to take off."

Garrett's eyes went wide. "Where the hell are you going?"

"Home. I'm not really into this."

"You, Nathan, have been my best mate since St Andrews, and you're not into this? What is going on?"

You've had her and now you want another taste. "I wish I could explain."

"Mate, I think this is Sophie. You've been spending a lot of your time with your neighbor lately."

Nathan ignored him. "No, it's not." It totally was. Because as much as he wanted to deny it, he would rather spend a day with her, than here, having conversations with beautiful but vapid blondes. "I'll check you later."

Within thirty minutes, he was charging up the stairs of his flat, and instead of going to his place, he went straight for Sophie's. When she opened the door, she looked beat up, exhausted and there were circles under her eyes. "Did I wake you?"

She shook her head. "No, I just feel like muck right now."

"Well, lucky for you I am here to cheer you up."

"I don't think there's anything you can do about this one."

He reached for her and gave her a cocky smirk. "Oh, I think I have a thing or two that can put you in a good mood."

Sophie shook her head. "No, not today."

He frowned. Was she ill? "What's wrong?"

She sighed. "If you really must know, I have my period. I've got cramps. I'm bloated. My feet hurt and I just want to have lie down. And or shoot someone, all the while I have the overwhelming urge to cry."

Her period. He frowned. This was one of the oddest conversations he'd ever had with a woman. But he could do this. He'd rather be with her than in his flat alone anyway. "What do you need?"

She gave him a weak smile. "Nathan, honestly, you're very sweet. But when I say I have my period I mean no fooling around. It does not mean it's blow job week for you."

He coughed a laugh. "Pity about the blow jobs, but I'm not that much of a twat. I know that. I'm just asking what you need. Whatever it is, I'll do it for you."

She studied him for a long moment. "Well, besides a foot massage, a tub of ice cream and to lay here on the couch doing absolutely nothing. Not much else. Wish I was more fun right now."

He just rolled his eyes before heading straight for her fridge. He pulled the ice cream out from the freezer, grabbed a couple of spoons from her drawers and then inclined his head toward the couch. When she tucked in next to him, he handed her the ice cream and then patted his lap. "Come on. Feet up."

"Are you serious right now?"

He nodded. "Yeah, I am *very* good with my hands." He waggled his eyebrows.

"Somehow I feel like I know this already."

He winked. "You should."

For the next couple of hours, they watched reality television and he massaged her feet. He would never tell Garrett this, but he was happier now than he'd been in the bar. Just having someone to talk to, someone who also smelled amazing. He liked talking to her. It calmed him down. And after that call with his father, he'd needed it.

When she finally fell asleep, he'd been loathe to let her go. But he pulled up the blanket and covered her before giving her a brief kiss on the forehead and heading back to his place.

Garrett was right. He had it bad. The problem was Sophie saw him as nothing more than fun and distraction. How the hell did he change her mind?

21

Was this what dating felt like? Nathan had never really done it before. Most of his life had been filled with sort of arranged relationship situations, with charities and functions, and being seen with the right people at the right time. So there were the women that he'd associated with for that.

Then there were the situations in the Uni years, where everyone was chatting up everyone else and things were fluid, and you were sort of just *with* someone. Even though he'd still been careful about entanglements. He'd had two relationships the whole time he'd been at St. Andrews. They had lasted a couple of months each. Both of the women were beautiful and fun, and it was nice having someone available to accompany him to St. Kitts on the odd weekend in Ibiza.

And then, he'd been out of university, and found it far easier to distance himself. The emotional drain wasn't anything he was looking for. The constant need for someone else's approval and attention wasn't really his thing. And it was easier to avoid getting hurt that way.

But what he had with Sophie right now? This odd friendship with incredible sex attached felt … amazing. The usual need he had to run away from emotional situations didn't occur with her. And then, of course, there were the lessons he was giving her on how to remain unattached and unemotional in romantic situations. *Yeah, because that seemed like a good idea at that time.*

But, the more he got to know her, the more time he spent with her doing things other than actively shagging, the more he liked her. And not in some sappy, he-wanted-to-marry-her kind of way, but in a way that spoke to the ease of being with her. If one of them didn't really feel like talking, they didn't really have to. They could watch a movie, or grab a drink, or even just sit there and read.

It had been a month since their arrangement began and more and more the thought of her taking everything he taught her and finding someone new made him twitchy.

I don't want that.

But he took those emotions and shoved them down. When did this happen? When had he broken his own rules and started to feel things? That wasn't part of the bargain. Honestly, he knew better. *Or at least you should have.*

Today he'd met her near Regent's Park for lunch. He'd anticipated some sit down at a restaurant, but oh no, she'd surprised him. She'd taken sandwiches and some drinks and had insisted they walked to the park. *Together.* The whole time they were walking and talking, he was so aware of her. All he wanted to do was touch her, and hold her, and —Shit. He was in trouble —so much trouble.

"What are you thinking about?"

"Nothing really. I was trying to figure out what your next lesson is going to be."

She was silent for a moment. "You know, I don't really think I need lessons anymore. You've already proven that the more aloof I am, the more detached I am, the more men find me appealing, which is disconcerting in so many ways, because honestly, why chase after someone who clearly isn't that into you?"

He chuckled. "Men are enigmas. Or, not really. What can I say? We like the chase. We like knowing we have to prove to you that we're worthy of your attention. For however long that might be. An hour, a day, a month, a year —whatever."

"So, what you're saying is that it's one big competition?"

He shrugged as he laughed. "Kind of, yeah. We are a bunch of twats, aren't we?"

Her peal of laughter made his gut clench. He watched her with her head thrown back and her hand wrapped around her middle even as she held her bag of sandwich and drink, and Jesus Christ, she was the most beautiful woman he had ever seen in his entire life.

"You're staring at me again. What, do I have food on my face?"

He considered telling her. Considered being honest. Just telling her what he was feeling and what he was thinking.

But you told her that this was no pressure. You told her this

was not going to happen. You warned her against this yourself.
What if she rejected him? What if she'd mastered the art of
nonemotional entanglements? What if he'd been *too* good of
a teacher?

"Nothing. I just like the red. It's like I'm sleeping with a
whole new woman."

She'd gone back to the hairdresser last week and gone
back to her natural color. She'd left a few blond highlights
and the overall effect was striking. It was like when he'd
seen her for the first time all over again. And these days,
instead of that sad, haunted woman, she was always
smiling around him. Always happy.

"No, you don't. Don't do that. What are you really
thinking?"

He wanted to tell her. It was on the tip of his tongue.
Imagine if he'd opened his mouth and just said, "I want
more with you"?

She would laugh. Or run. He wasn't going to let either
of those two happen. "No, I'm serious. You look incredibly
sexy. I can't believe that wanker told you to go blond. Come
on, let's sit over there."

He led her over to one of the benches and they sat and
had their lunch. It was better that he didn't tell her. Better
that he got his emotions under control. Because the alternative meant he was going to get hurt. Or worse, that he
would eventually hurt her and that was the one thing he
couldn't allow.

~

"I MUST SAY, I was skeptical, but the two of you seem to have this whole, like, friends and benefits thing going pretty well." Gemma appraised Nathan even as she gave Sophie a light shoulder shove. Her gaze slid over Garrett following that and she said, "Maybe you and I should try it?"

Garrett downed his drink and flashed her a grin. "I have been hoping you would say that. Why don't you and I get the shagging bit out now and then we can work on being friends later?"

Gemma just rolled her eyes. "Nathan, how come all your friends aren't as enlightened as you?"

Nathan laughed. "What can I say? I'm an evolved kind of man."

Sophie watched the banter between everyone and she had to smile to herself. She liked this. She *liked* him. Who was she kidding? She was totally falling for him. Every day was a struggle not to show her emotions. To not show how she was feeling, and to not tip him off, because if she did, then he would stop. The lessons would stop. Their time together would stop.

The nights they just sat around watching movies and drinking wine would stop. So never mind that she, like the idiot she was, had fallen in love with the guy who was too rich and too good-looking for his own good. Yeah, never mind that. He thought they were just friends. *Imagine that.*

She leaned forward. "He's not *that* enlightened. I keep waiting for him to run like a little jackrabbit. I'm just waiting to see when his experiment ends."

The smile he gave her was teasing, but she saw that it

didn't reach his eyes. *Shit*, had she said something wrong? When he spoke, his tone was light. "Well, you keep doing that thing that you do, you know, when I'm between your —"

"Nathan, stop it." She gave him her very stern look, even as she fought a laugh. And this time, the smile reached his eyes. And with that classic Nathan Windsor smile, heat flooded to her center. Yes, this was completely unhealthy. Yes, she was going to get hurt. But it was the most fun she'd had in any of her relationships. She was happy. And she didn't want it to end. So, she just wasn't going to rock the boat. She wasn't going to let him see.

"I mean, honestly, Sophie, you could give a class. I mean the way you —"

She clasped a hand over his mouth. And he kissed her fingers while he winked at her.

"Nathan Windsor, if you so much as say a word, you will be in so much trouble."

Gemma leaned forward, interested. "Are you gonna spank him?"

Garrett guffawed. Nathan nearly choked on the scotch.

Sophie shook her head. "You three are impossible. I'll be right back." She scooted off her stool and headed back to the throngs of people toward the loop. She needed a moment away from him —a moment to tamp down the fear and to get herself under control so that she wouldn't blurt out, "I'm in love with you, Nathan."

When she reached the loo, she gave herself the once-over in the mirror and gave herself the same speech she'd been giving on repeat for weeks. "You cannot be in love with him. He made it very, very clear. So, get your shit together."

There was nothing like a good old pep talk to knock some sense into her. *Liar.*

On the way back to the table, she bumped into someone tall and broad shouldered. "Sorry, it's really crowded in here." When he turned around, she realized he looked familiar. "Have I seen you before?"

He grinned down on her. "Isn't that supposed to be my line?" He was definitely her type. Good looking, a couple of tattoos, stubble, emotionally unavailable. Now where had she seen him before?

"Yes, I suppose that is supposed to be your line."

"Actually, you do look familiar. How about I take you out, and we can figure out where we know each other from? What's your name?"

"Hi, I'm Sophie."

"Hi Sophie. I'm Adam. I think we actually met at a bar a couple of months ago."

She frowned and slid her gaze over him. "Oh God, yeah." At one of the first nights of her lessons with Nathan. "Okay, yeah, yeah. I remember now. How's it going?"

"Better now. So, about that date —"

Her gazed looked past him over to Nathan, Gemma, and Garrett. That was what she wanted. Her boyfriend and his friend getting along with her best friend. She wanted that. But, Nathan had been very, very clear. That's not what they were. She couldn't have that with him. And the whole point was, she was supposed to learn how to have fun and date and not get herself hurt. So, she would need practical application, wouldn't she? "Um, well, the thing is —"

"Let me guess: boyfriend?"

She looked on over at the table again. "Actually, no. No boyfriend. It's a complicated thing but no boyfriend."

"In that case, I won't take no for an answer. We can even just go out as friends. See if you like me, and I think you will. See if it's worth complicating your life with your, uh, complication."

"I'm not sure. You know, I —I'd better — "

"Say yes. Just meet me at the bar that we met at. Give me your number. We'll set up a drink. A drink between friends even and we'll see."

He took out his mobile and waited expectantly for her to rattle off her number. When she did, he gave her a grin. And then her phone buzzed in her hand.

Unknown Number: You have my number now.

She smirked. "I guess I have your number now too."

"That you do. Best program my name in. I will definitely be calling you, Sophie."

She smiled up at him. He really was very good-looking. Just not the one she wanted. *Which is why you still need to go out with him.* "Well, I look forward to hearing from you, Adam."

When she slid back onto her stool, Nathan gave her a once-over. "All right?"

"Yep, perfect. Some guy just asked me out."

Immediately, she could see his eyes go blank, even though he gave her a wide smile. "See, confidence shows through. Where's the lucky bloke taking you?"

"Just for a drink or whatever. We'll see if he calls. I get the impression he's just trying to see how many he can pull tonight."

Nathan took a long swig of his drink. "Oh, I promise you. He'll call. He sees what I do."

She didn't know what she was waiting for: a streak of jealousy —something. Either way, it didn't come. And that hurt. It meant when Adam did call, she absolutely needed to take it and go on that date because the thing she had with Nathan was only going to get them hurt —her especially.

22

As it turned out, Adam did call. Well, texted. Sophie had even shown the text message to her coach. "What does this even mean?"

She'd been in the middle of an event when she'd gotten the text. One she'd invited Nathan to because well, he was Nathan Windsor, and he could go to any event he wanted, so she might as well have him close since they were friends. And as it was, she now needed him. "It just says, 'How about that drink?'"

Nathan slid his gaze over her. "Well, Sophie, it means how about that drink?"

She narrowed her gaze at him. "You are being deliberately obtuse. And because I'm working, I can't smack you for it."

He chuckled. "No, you can't. You have to be the picture of decorum, whereas I can be a complete letch."

She giggled. "Seriously, you're like six months older than I am."

"That's exactly right. You are the younger woman here. I want to teach you *all* the things."

She laughed even as she slid her gaze around, making sure that no one could hear them. "You want to teach me all the naked things."

"I teach you these things out of love."

Right at that moment, her boss, Allison, came up and Sophie had to pretend that her body wasn't flooded with heat. "Sophie, oh my God, the client is so happy. You've outdone yourself this time. Even with a minimal budget, look at what you've been able to pull off. The Dawstons are so happy with what you did for their friend and they decided to match the entire charitable contribution."

Sophie beamed. "Oh my God, that's amazing." Even though this event technically wasn't with Glass Slipper Events, she'd still had Allison. She wanted her feedback.

"You keep up this kind of work and I might have to open a charity arm to the events business. Seriously, you did a great job." She nodded a greeting to Nathan and then floated off to the crowd.

Sophie beamed at Nathan who gave her a wide smile. "You did a great job. She's right. Now, since the client is happy, and since they got extra money, I say it's time to be naughty."

"Nathan, the event is not over. I can't just leave."

"Everything is under control, and you're not leaving. I know you'll stay 'til the end to make sure everyone's cleaning up, but I have been wanting to celebrate. Come with me."

He led her through the crowd, out the barroom and

headed to the left. Then they took a side-winding staircase up a floor. "Nathan, I don't think we're supposed to be up here."

His gaze was hot, intent. "You've always done what you're supposed to do?"

Simple answer: yes. Always. Maybe he was right. Maybe it was time to be naughty. "Yes, always. Maybe it's time I change that."

"Now that is what I'm talking about, Sophie."

Nathan tugged her into a room. The lights were low and it looked like a sitting room for one of the many functions thrown here. "Nathan, what are we doing here?"

"Be quiet so I can show you." The scorching kiss he slanted over her mouth sizzled her synapses.

Sophie dragged him to her by his velvet suit jacket. She slid her arms inside to the shoulders, dropping it off him smoothly.

Nathan spun them both around and flattened her against a wall, wholly devouring her lips. He licked inside her mouth as his hips ground into her. Through his pants, his cock burned hot against her belly. Impatient, she quickly unbuttoned his shirt, dragged it out of his pants, and placed her hand on his abs.

His muscles contracted with every flutter of her fingertips and he murmured hot, dirty words against her lips, driving her crazy with his need, his urgency. This was the Nathan she craved. The raw and hungry Nathan. The one who always seemed to want her. In moments like this, she could believe he was falling for her. And right about now, she needed the fantasy.

Sophie traced a path from his chest to the light trail of hair just above his pants. She went for the button, and his hand snapped to hers to stay it. He didn't so much stop her as guide her. Unsure what to do, she stayed perfectly still for several seconds as he continued to kiss her. This whole thing was so bloody fucked up, but she needed him.

When he didn't move her hand, Sophie tucked her palm under his and guided them into his pants. As she closed her fingers around the rigid length of him, his hand closed over hers. In tandem, they stroked him from base to tip. He showed her how to tease the tip, how to hold the base steady and allow more blood to flow into his cock. He even guided her hand down to his balls and taught her how to pay homage to them. She used the tip of her finger to tease his perineum, and he swore savagely.

"Jesus, Sophie."

She pressed gently again, and his knees buckled.

His voice was low and strained against her ear. "I don't want to come until I'm buried deep inside you. But you keep that up, I'm not going to make it another second."

Reluctantly, she withdrew her hand, and he followed suit. Nuzzling her neck, he then whispered, "Turn around."

She met his gaze and searched it. Not sure where this was going to go, she complied.

"Good. Now place your hands against the door."

Her hands shaking, she did as he told her. Uncertain, she looked over her shoulder. He was examining the fabric of her dress. Quickly, he grabbed fistfuls of it and dragged it upward, exposing her bare arse to the cool draft.

"Fuck, Sophie, why aren't you wearing knickers?"

Her voice shook as she spoke. "Well, I figured it was just one more layer that you'd rip off anyway."

"And you would be right about that." His voice was a growl against her ear. He gave her a brief swat on her arse and she moaned. It surprised more than it hurt.

"I'm not feeling particularly patient right now with you, so good thinking."

"Nathan, I need you."

Nathan placed an open-mouthed kiss in the crook between her neck and shoulder. He nipped her skin then soothed the nips with tiny licks. His hands reached up to her breasts, and circled her nipples with his thumbs, his forefinger and thumb tugging lightly. Sophie moaned. Eventually, as he kissed the nape of her neck, he abandoned that idea and tugged down the top of the dress, exposing her fully.

"Do you have any fucking idea how beautiful you are? So gorgeous. It's been work trying to keep my hands to myself all night."

As one hand caressed her arse, the other slipped around her waist, then down between her thighs. Teasing her slick lips for just a moment, he then slid two fingers into her wet center. Sophie gritted her teeth against the onslaught of need. Only Nathan could give her what she craved. Only Nathan could give her what she wanted. He sank his finger deep, and then stroked her inside and out gently. Teasing her, bringing her almost to the heights of pleasure, then bringing her back from the brink. Then back again.

Through a fog of lust, Sophie heard the rip of foil. In

another second, the thick, hard length of him pressed inside her slick entrance.

"Brace your arms, Sophie. Spread your legs, baby. Wider. Yeah, like that."

When he slid in to the hilt, Sophie cried out. Nathan bit her shoulder as he clamped one hand on her hip. All the while he used the thumb from his free hand to tease that forbidden place. He'd taken to doing that more and more when they had sex.

She knew what was coming. What he was preparing her for. And it excited her. It also terrified her because he was so big. "You like this Sophie, don't you?"

She groaned as he claimed her. "Y—yes, Nathan."

He gave her a frustrated growl. "You think anyone else can make you feel like this?"

"No, God, no. Nathan, please. I need to—"

"You think your ex boyfriend can make you feel like this?"

"N—no. Oh God."

He set a bruising pace, but she met him thrust for thrust. She needed his brand on her, all over her. She could pretend she was his. Pretend that he wanted more from her. Pretend that the way he was tonight, desperate and barely restrained, was fueled by jealousy and need.

As he sank into her over and over again, Sophie called out his name again and again. "Nathan, Nathan, Nathan."

The tingle in her toes started just before he brought a hand around to dip between her thighs and stroke her clit. Sophie's body shook as she came apart in his hands. He followed her quickly with one more thrust before he stiffened behind her. He whispered her name and kissed the column of her neck. "So beautiful."

He carefully slid out of her and cleaned up. Sophie leaned against the wall, panting. In all her years dating, had she felt anything like this? God, no. And when she finally found something like this, it was with a man she shouldn't want.

After he'd rearranged his clothes, he helped her adjust hers. Her hair was ravaged, so she let it tumble down around her shoulders. No point in trying to pretend the fancy updo was going to hold.

Before he could lead her out the door, she tugged him back. "Nathan?"

"Yeah, beautiful?"

"What are we doing?"

His smile was easy and quick, but something about it didn't quite reach his eyes. "We're having fun. Being spontaneous, right?"

She nodded slowly before she let him take her back to the party. Before she could feel put out about his response, he held on to her hand tightly, making it difficult for anyone watching not to have an idea of what they'd been up to.

"You finish up. Then when we get back, I'll show you a few more dirty things I want to do to you."

Oh shit. She should be terrified, but she wasn't.

For the first time in her life, she felt comfortable, like she belonged where she was. But for how long?

23

Sophie smiled down at the text.

Nathan: Come to Ivy and Thorn. It's lonely drinking without you. Besides, you need practice.

The word *practice*. God, she hated that word. She didn't want any more practice. She wanted to be with him. *Easy does it. You guys are not a thing. It's casual.*

Yes, it was casual. She knew that. It was just fun being with him and she liked having fun. Not having to be so serious all the time. It was exhausting. With Nathan she felt light, freer. Wanting to be a glutton for punishment, she immediately ran into her bedroom, swung open her closet doors and tried to find something that was sexy, sleek, and sophisticated but also like she wasn't trying too hard. She finally settled on a pair of leather skinny pants. Honestly, the effort required to tug these things on might not be worth it, but Nathan would see her in them and probably decide that she needed another lesson on orgasms, which she was totally okay with. She tugged them on and then sent him a quick message back.

"Okay, on my way. Have good news too."

That was as much as she let herself divulge. That was cool. That was casual, right? *You are setting yourself up for pain.* No, she wasn't. This was casual. And honestly, she hadn't quite had her fill of casual and fun. She could have more casual and fun. At least until she met the next guy, the real Mr. Right. Nathan made her feel good. That was all. She was not developing soft love for him. Especially not after the other night when he rubbed her feet, gave her a hot water bottle and then covered her with a blanket when she fell asleep. And he hadn't even gotten anything out of the deal except to watch movies.

In under thirty minutes, she was dressed, had a light dusting of makeup on, her good bra that made her boobs actually look like they were the same size, and perfumed in secret hidden spots, that he would hopefully find later. Not that she was getting dressed up for him. She was getting dressed up for herself. Not necessarily Nathan.

For a guy who spent a lot of time training her on how to talk to men, and how to be the hottest woman in the room, he spent a lot of time cock blocking her too. Maybe he just wanted to see his lessons in practice. The flare of hope was swift and immediate and she shut it down with such force and immediacy that she staggered. No, not him. He was fun. Besides she knew what it was like to be with men like that. It would be nothing but heartbreak. She took one last glance at the mirror. Perfect. And she tried like hell to not be excited that she was going to see him.

It took less than ten minutes to arrive at the Ivy and
Vine. She gave her name and was immediately able to
bypass the long queue that had started to form at the door.
Her blood rushed, thumping in time to the beat. It was
nice to be out for once and not be working. She was excited,
her good news brimming over. *Stop kidding yourself. You're
just excited to see him.*

Yes, she was. God, she hoped it wasn't obvious.

When she saw him, she froze in her tracks. There was a
gorgeous blonde wrapped around him. Standing in front of
him and then eventually straddling his thighs. Nathan, for
his part, leaned back for a moment. But then she said something and he leaned forward and gave her that look. Sophie
had seen that look before. That had been the same one he'd
given to her when he wanted to fuck her.

Shit. She'd gotten this all wrong. How the hell had that
happened? *Because you allowed yourself to believe that you
could be with a guy like that. That for once, somebody like that
would choose you.* Well, she'd been wrong about that.

The problem was, she turned away a moment too late.
The blond woman moved her head to the side and Sophie
and Nathan made eye contact for the barest hint of a
moment. But in the next second, Sophie was leaving out the
door, quick as a flash. She'd let her imagination take over
and she could almost pretend she heard him calling after
her to stop, to wait for him. But she knew that was a lie.

THE STATUESQUE BLONDE leaned into Nathan's side. Instinct

had him recoiling away from her a step. Somewhere along the line, other women had become repelling magnets to him.

She frowned as she studied him closely. "You're jumpy tonight. I swear Nathan, we haven't had one of our usual sessions in weeks. It's like you've lost my number or something. Now you're acting like you're not happy to see me."

Ilsa. Beautiful. Accomplished even. Mouth like a hoover. Problem was, in the last few weeks or so he hadn't been really particularly interested in seeing her. What they had wasn't even casual. If he needed a date and felt like it, he called her. And usually, he felt like it at least a couple of times a month but not since Sophie. Not since he'd seen her get her heart twisted up. Since then, he had been all Sophie, all the time. He hadn't even thought of Ilsa once. "Ilsa, you look well."

She tsked and wound her arms like two boa constrictors around his neck. "Don't give me the 'you-look-well.' Where have you been? I thought you and I had a good thing going?"

With practiced ease he extricated himself from her hold. She'd been drinking. And she was prone to scenes when she was drinking. And there it was. What he was constantly trying to avoid: Attachment. Connection.

Connection isn't a problem if it came from Sophie. Fuck, he had it so bad. "You know how it is. I've been busy." Was he supposed to have officially called it off with Ilsa? Hell he'd never been in this position before. What the hell was the damn protocol?

"I can see that. But you haven't even called me for any of

the charity functions you've attended this month. I saw your photo in the society pages."

Fuck him. That was how this whole thing had even started. She had been the perfect date. Someone who presented well amongst investors, would fit in that part of society, but then would also understand that just because he shagged her didn't mean that they were together.

Hell, she'd suggested they be each other's casual-consistent plus ones in the first place. It had been a win-win with the occasional night together thrown in. There was no permanence to it. She'd just come to expect the occasional call for a charity function or two.

He wasn't looking for anyone, and she was looking for an older rich husband to spoil her. What they had was less than casual. But now, that noose felt too tight. "I'm sorry, Ilsa. Maybe we can meet another time for tea or something."

She narrowed her gaze on him. "Tea? Nathan, that positively sounds like a brush off." Bugger. He was going to have to do the whole sit down break it off thing, wasn't he? Even though they'd never been anything.

And that's because it was a brush off. Over Ilsa's shoulder, he could see Garrett chuckling into his drink. "Ilsa, look we'll talk about this another time. I'm waiting for someone. And you've been drinking."

She blinked rapidly. "Stop being a spoilsport. I'm not trying to rope you down. I just miss you, that's all. How's this: why don't you go ahead and give me a call in the next couple of weeks or so? I can maybe remind you of why we're so good together."

It was official the old Nathan Windsor was dead. He'd

been body snatched. Because the suggestion of being with her again left him cold. It was simple. She wasn't Sophie. And there would be no gently letting down. It was going to have to happen here. "Actually, Ilsa our arrangement no longer works for me."

Her eyes went wide and filled with tears. *Shit.* He was not equipped for tears. And he saw now, she had hoped to parlay their casual situation into making him her rich husband. *Sorry, someone already beat you to it.*

"Oh, come on Nathan, don't be like that." She turned to Garrett. "Tell him to calm down. We're just having fun. I'm teasing him."

Garrett shook his head. "Leave me out of this."

She turned back to Nathan and looped her hands around his neck, bringing her lips dangerously close. He pulled back, reaching behind his neck to unclasp her hands. "That's enough, Ilsa." He didn't want her hands on him. At the same time, he didn't want to physically harm her.

Unfortunately, she took his gentleness as playing hard to get and she jumped in his lap. "Nathan, are you really going to tell me you don't want me? You and I have a good thing going."

"No. We don't." He applied more pressure to her fingers and cursed with she winced, but he managed to restraint both of her hands together and angle his head away. If he pushed her he was afraid she'd fall on those teetering heels of hers. "Not interested, Ilsa. Now, get—"

He felt it then. A hot lick of desire went up his spine. Immediately, his gaze sought out Sophie. She was here, and they—

"Ilsa, get off." He set her away from him as gently as he could, but she still went sprawling. And worse, Sophie was already flying out the door. "Garrett, get the bill. Deal with Ilsa. I have to go." He helped Ilsa to her feet, then passed her on to Garret and hustled for the door.

Garrett looked towards the door and shook his head. "Hurry, mate."

"On it." The panic sat and enclosed around him. He had to get to Sophie.

Oh shit, he had fucked up so badly. What the fuck had he been letting Ilsa get so close? He'd seen Sophie a moment too late, as he'd been in the midst getting rid of Ilsa. What had she seen? Had she thought … ? *Not that it matters because you two aren't together. What you have is casual.* Or was it? Of course, it was completely casual. *Oh yeah? Then why are you panicked right now?*

He'd run out of the club after her, but she'd gotten in a cab immediately. He'd had to wait an additional ten minutes. Of course he kept calling, but she kept ending the call. Damn it. He so fucked up. How the hell was he ever going to explain that he hadn't been up to anything with Ilsa? That he'd been breaking off their semi-casual situation because he wanted Sophie to take him seriously? Shit, he wanted her to more than take him seriously. He wanted her. Pressing, rude, or whatever, she was the one he wanted. When he finally reached the flat, he circumvented the cue of partygoers at the club downstairs and went to the side entrance. He didn't bother to wait for the elevator but instead took the stairs two at a time, running all the way to her flat.

He banged on it hard. No response. He could sort of hear voices inside like she had the television on. Damn it. She wasn't going to open the door. "Damn it Sophie, it wasn't what you thought. Let me in."

It took several moments until she finally answered the door. Her face was devoid of makeup and she'd already changed into her sweatpants and a T-shirt. He was so relieved to see her. "Sophie, look, I know what it looked like."

She sighed. Exhaustion made her look tired. "Nathan, it doesn't matter. Honestly. I screwed up. I know it. This is my fault. What is happening is my responsibility."

He frowned. "What the hell? Sophie, listen, I know I cocked up, okay? I'm sorry. It wasn't what it looked like. I swear. I don't know what happened. I just—"

"I know what happened. She was beautiful. Completely into you, and easy— which is fine, because you made it perfectly clear what your ideal is. I was the one who messed up here. I knew that. I accept it."

He searched her face and he wished he could make her understand. He wished he could make her see. "You didn't mess up, Sophie. I did. From the beginning, I didn't want something casual. I—"

"You have a funny way of showing it. And I know who you are. Even if I thought I was developing feelings for you, I know who you are. You have always been clear about that. I'm the one who didn't listen. Instinct. Intuition. All of it. I just—I didn't listen. And right now, that hurts. It was a painful lesson to learn, but I have learned it now."

Fuck. Fuck. Fuck. This was going all wrong. "I am sorry.

She was all over me. I pushed her off. Please, let's just talk about this. I don't want to lose you."

"Lose me? You and I both know what this is. We were friends who fucked. And now we're not."

His brows snapped down. "We're not friends, or we're not fucking anymore?"

"I think it's probably better if we're not friends." And then she quietly shut the door in his face.

In a span of seconds, he'd lost her.

24

Gemma answered on the first ring. "Hey ya love. How come you're not all loved up with your not-quite-boyfriend?"

Sophie swiped the tears off her cheek with the back of her hand. "Because my not-quite-boyfriend was all over some blonde today. So that's done."

Gemma cursed. "I'll be there in a tick."

Her best friend wasn't kidding. Less than ten minutes later, she was knocking on Sophie's door. When Sophie opened it, Gemma immediately wrapped her in the warm cocoon of a hug. "That twat. I'll kill him. Is he home?" she started to yell but Sophie stopped her.

"Stop it. I don't—I don't want him to know I'm upset. I just—I knew it was a mistake, and I did it anyway. Now—" Her shoulders shook and the tears just flowed. "Now it's all fucked up and I feel like I have lost my best friend, and it's awful."

Gemma snapped her hands onto her hips. "First of all,

you haven't lost your best friend; I'm standing right here. And I resent the fact that he thought he could take my place. Second of all, you know you can do better than him, right? I mean, yeah, he's fit and all that, but there are better guys out there. Ones that deserve you. Ones that will treat you like a queen. Fuckwits like Christopher and Nathan can go eat a bowl of dicks. Okay?"

Sophie nodded trying to convince herself that Gemma was right. She didn't need Nathan. She was just fine without him.

Why did this hurt so badly? It never ceased to amaze her how that horrible pit-in-the-stomach-feeling felt like. Like she was falling off a cliff and there was no way to stop it.

"I just—I don't know. I made a mistake. It was my fault. I—I convinced myself that I didn't care, that I could just do this fun thing, and apparently I can't because, God it hurts so bad."

Gemma set about with the heartache remedy. She had Sophie ensconced on the couch with a duvet wrapped around her and *Downton Abbey* on the telly. And then she brought over the wine, the corkscrew, a tub of cookies and cream ice cream, and teaspoons. "You and I will get through this together. Now, tell me what the hell happened? The last time I saw the two of you, I would have sworn he was in love with you. I mean, just the way he looked at you. Every second you left the table, his eyes tracked where you were going. This doesn't make sense."

"That's just the thing, right? He's so charming and so good you believe it. You'd completely buy his whole act.

And there I was buying everything. Just like he warned me against. I mean, the guy gave me the blueprint and told me not to fall for it. He told me not to get caught up. And what did I do? I got caught up. I seriously need to have my head examined."

"Now love, you don't need your head examined. I mean, who isn't going to fall for the gorgeous, charming bloke who acts like he absolutely adores you? I'd have been victim too."

"The operative word there being 'acts like.'"

Gemma took a swig of the wine because after all, who needed glasses? "Okay, hear me out, but maybe it wasn't what you thought, you know, with the girl. You saw how angry he was about what Christopher did to you. And you know that that's his trigger. I honestly am not sure if he would really be trying it on with someone after he told you to come out."

"I didn't really give him a chance to explain because even though that's his huge problem and it hurts seeing him like that, the real problem is that it felt that way. That it hurts so much. If that's not a reason to stop this whole scenario, then I don't know what is."

Gemma nodded. "I hear you. It's just—You guys seemed to be genuinely happy together, like two peas in a pod. You finish each other's sentences even. I know you've become very close. I'm sorry it hurt so much."

"Yeah, me too. And now, I have to endure living across the hall from him and hearing about all his sexual adventures. This is going to be fantastic. I'll be bloody torturing myself for the next six months."

Gemma put the bottle down and glared at her. "Oh no, you shall not stay in this flat and wallow. We are going to go out. As you know, the best way to get over someone is to get under someone else. So that very cute guy that gave you his number? We're going to call him."

Sophie shifted uncomfortably in the couch. "I don't know. He did text about meeting at the bar, but I think maybe I should have a break from men, you know?"

"I hear you, but first you get over the sex god across the hall and then you take a break from men. You can't try and go cold turkey like that. It, like, breaks your vagina or something."

Sophie sputtered a laugh. "Are you serious right now? It's going to break my vagina?"

Gemma nodded sagely. "I've heard that's how it happens. You just got to get this one to add to your system. Shag some new bloke. And once Arsehole Neighbor across the Hall isn't the last guy you shag, then it won't hurt so bad to see him."

Sophie frowned at her best friend. Maybe that wasn't the worst idea Gemma had had after all.

Why was she shaking? *You knew the deal. You knew this was casual. You two don't mean anything to each other.*

The problem was she believed that they were at least friends. He was supposed to tell her first. Supposed to let her know. *Liar.* She started to believe that something was happening with them. That things weren't just friendly or casual. She'd gone ahead and fallen in love with the player. That's why this hurt so badly. That's why this felt like her gut had been ripped out. It hurt, and it was her own fault.

You should know better than anyone. Just because somebody says the right things doesn't mean you can believe them. There was a reason she didn't date guys like Nathan. There was a reason she didn't date guys that were too good-looking for words. There would always be someone more beautiful waiting in the wings, someone else to take their attention away. There would always be some reason they would disappoint you.

The first, hot splash of a tear fell on her cheek and she swiped it away angrily. No, she was not going to cry.

She made a mistake. Everyone made mistakes, her included. She could remedy this mistake. She'd already started making changes in her life. It was fine. She knew what to do. She'd already taken the first steps today. Her whole afternoon had been great. And of course, like a fool, the first person she'd wanted to tell was Nathan. That was her bad. She started to rely on him. Well, no more. She knew better.

"I was so stupid."

Gemma rubbed her back. "No, you weren't. You were just falling for him. That's all. It's okay. He's just not the settling down type. There are plenty of blokes who are. What happened to that one who chatted you up the night we all went out? He was well fit. Besides, it's better that you try dating someone else any way. After all that shit with your dad, and that wanker Christopher and now Nathan. I think maybe you just need a bloke who's really into you and will shower you with affection right now. You know someone who's more into you than you are into him."

Sophie swallowed hard. She did not want to think about

going out with anyone else at the moment. She was really off men. But Gemma had a point. She'd had a run of bad luck. "Not going to happen. Look, I have a solution to my bad luck. I'm going to join a convent."

Gemma coughed. "No can do, love. They won't let you sneak battery operated boyfriend into the nunnery. Though I'm sure the sisters could use it. You're just reeling from a shitty situation. No need to be extreme."

"I'm not being extreme. I mean, I keep thinking I've found these great blokes. Hell, Christopher was perfect on paper. See how well that turned out. And Nathan, well he was just Nathan. So here I am again. Alone."

Gemma gave her a gentle squeeze. "Right. That's enough of the pity party. I'm going to solve this problem."

"I already told you, castrating him would only offer me temporary solace."

"No, better than that. They say the best way to get over someone is to get under someone else."

"The last thing I need is another dick in my life."

"I disagree. That's exactly what you need." Gemma grabbed her mobile and Sophie tried to wrestle it back, but Gemma was deceptively strong. She put the phone on speaker as it rang. The two rapid rings followed by silence, then another ring, when a man on the other end finally answered, he sounded like he was in the car. "Hullo? Sophie?"

Oh shit. She'd called fit Adam. Sophie was going to kill her. Right after the ground opened and swallowed her whole.

With a glare for her bestie, she said, "Hi, Adam. How's it?"

"GREAT NOW. Listen I was just thinking of you actually. Wondering when would be not too soon to ask you for drinks."

"I uh—" she was on the verge of declining when Gemma glared at her. Her bestie did have a point. It was just a drink. She could do that. Besides, anything was better than sitting around waiting for the nonstop sex party to start again. "Yeah—of course," she sputtered. "When?"

"Tomorrow night? The bar where we met? It's Sunday, it'll be quieter."

"Yeah, sure."

"It's a date." He was silent for a moment, then added, "Sophie, I'm glad you called."

She ignored that little voice in her head that told her she was making a mistake. Anything had to be better than how she was feeling now.

25

The next night, Sophie still wasn't sure she'd made the right decision, but she was trying to go with it.

"I'm really excited you gave me a chance. Honestly, I didn't think you'd call."

Sophie shifted on her boot-clad feet. Adam, he was nice. He seemed really cool actually. And to be fair, she didn't really have anything else going on. So, it didn't hurt to catch a drink with him.

"Well, you were very sweet. So, I figured why not?"

"Well, I'm glad. You want to grab a drink here before we go on down?" He shrugged. "I figured instead of just drinks, we'd get dinner too."

"Yeah, I don't really have anything up here except for cheap wine. I hope that's okay."

He shrugged. "To be perfectly honest, I know nothing about wine. I'm always amused by, you know, these twats you hear on a date waxing poetic about what wine is better with what and what you must have and all that bullshit. I honestly don't like wine. I'm not really a beer drinker either. If I'm drinking, it'll be liquor, but you can't really tell your mates you're not going to sit and have a Guinness with them."

She laughed. "How many pints have you sacrificed yourself for just to appear cool with your mates?"

He shook his head as he laughed. "Far too many."

"Let me just grab my—"

There was a knock at the door and she jogged to get it. When she opened it, she stopped short. "Nathan, what are you doing here?"

He shrugged, but his narrow-eyed gaze landed directly on Adam. "Well, I was coming to tell you that there was a leak in one of the pipes. The building manager called me and said we shouldn't experience any flooding except maybe in the hallway. So, I was coming to notify you of that. I didn't know you were occupied."

Shit. This was hard enough. Why couldn't she just have made it out of the house without actually having to see him? *Well, because the whole make-the-guy-jealous thing, only actually works if he sees who you're dating.* But to be honest, it's not like she was dating here. She pulled back a little. "Thanks for letting me know."

"Are you going to introduce me to your friend?"

Adam sauntered over with a wide grin and a cocky swagger. "Mate, I'm Adam."

He stuck his hand out to shake Nathan's and Sophie watched in fascination as they sized each other up.

Nathan nodded. "I'm Nathan Winsor. Sophie's …neighbor."

They both glared at each other for a moment. Finally, Adam gave Nathan a wide grin. "We've actually met before at the bar downstairs. You spilled your drink down my back."

Nathan's gaze narrowed. "Oh right. Wish I could say I was sorry, but you were hitting on my girl."

Adam's grin just stretched across his handsome face. "Is that so? It looks like your girl is going on a date with me tonight. How does that make you feel?"

Nathan's jaw ticked.

"Well, this is fun but Sophie and I have a date. So ... "

Sophie immediately stepped between the two of them. "Nathan, thank you for letting me know. But I'm afraid we have to get going."

"Are you seriously dating this guy?"

Sophie glared at him, and she refused to acknowledge his question. "Goodbye, Nathan."

But Nathan wasn't having it. When she tried to close the door, he wedged his foot inside the door.

Sophie met his gaze directly. "Nathan, I need to go now."

Everything about Nathan said he had no intention of letting go. But then something in his eyes shuttered and he stepped back. "Well, I guess you guys go have fun."

When she closed the door, she sagged against it, closing her eyes for a moment. When was this feeling going to go away? When was she going to start to feel better?

"Are you honestly shagging that guy?"

Sophie turned on Adam. "Look, it's complicated. We were friends. Now we're not, as you can see."

He grinned. "It's fine. It's his loss, my gain."

"Well, let's go have that drink and then we'll see."

He sighed. "So, you were into him then?"

How was she supposed to answer that? Honestly. "It's a long story. It didn't end well, but I'm not interested in shagging him anymore." *What happened to the truth? You were doing so well with it.* "I'm not trying to have anything complicated. I just want to be free as a bird and see where the waters take me. Besides, it's not that simple. As of right now, we're not shagging. We're not even friends, which makes me sad. So, I'm just trying to get myself out there and do me."

He shook his head. "I guess I lost my shot. I shouldn't have gotten your number when I first saw you at the bar."

"What do you mean?"

He laughed. "Sophie, you're clearly really into him. And he is clearly in love with you."

"You don't know that."

He shrugged. "I know a thing or two about guys."

"And I guess I don't—which is why I'm feeling like this. I'm the idiot who fell in love."

Adam chuckled. "From the look in his eyes, you're not the only one who fell in love."

26

"You look like shit, mate."

Nathan still wasn't sure why he'd opened the door for Garrett. Maybe it was because his best mate had threatened to call over every single woman in the bar downstairs to cheer him up if he hadn't. But still, Nathan was regretting it. "Yeah, thanks. You know, I didn't ask you to come over. You can go."

"Oh, stop being like that. I haven't seen you in days. You bought a theater. You don't tell me anything about it. There are papers to be signed. You're off, Nathan. What's the matter?"

Nathan ran his hand through his hair. "I fucked up with the whole Ilsa thing."

Garrett cursed under his breath. "Ilsa was just being Ilsa. Besides, I thought the whole thing with Sophie was that you guys were friends. It didn't really matter."

"Yeah well, that was all fine before I fell in love with her. That was all fun until I started feeling things."

Garrett's brows lifted. "Things?"

"Fuck, I don't know how to explain it."

Garrett nodded wisely. "Well, sometimes when boys like girls, funny feelings happen in their—"

"Shut it."

Garrett chuckled. "I mean, Sophie's hot. But why is she any more special than anyone else?"

"I don't know. I like this one. She's smart and funny, and —I don't know. Somewhere along the line she wormed her way under my skin and I couldn't shake her and—"

"And this is why you don't shag your friends."

Nathan scoffed. "I'm in no hurry to shag you."

Garrett gave him a once-over. "Please. I have better taste in guys. You have to buy me a lot of dinners first."

Nathan just rolled his eyes.

"Nathan, if it's upsetting you this much, go talk to her. At least that way we can get rid of this grumpy sack of shit that you're calling your face right now."

"What, you think I'm not bright enough to try to talk to her? Hell, I went over there tonight. She's on a fucking date."

Garrett winced. "Oh, that's rough."

"Tell me about it. She wouldn't even hear a word I had to say."

Garrett nodded. "The thing is, you've managed your whole life to go without actually caring about anyone besides you know, your mum and Judith. Yeah, sure, mates and such, but real feelings? You always hold yourself back. And the thing is, with her feelings, she's entitled to feel them. I'm sure it sucked seeing you with Ilsa. I'm sure she didn't like seeing someone with her hands all over you."

"I wasn't doing anything. And I was actively trying to get her off of me."

Garrett held up his hands. "Yes, of course, because any idiot can see how in love with Sophie you are. I'm just saying that if you look at things from her eyes, it probably looks like the same old Nathan. So, you're going to have to let her be entitled to her feelings, and just keep trying."

"How did you get so fucking wise?"

His best friend cleared his throat. "I've had my heart broken before, you know."

Nathan frowned. How had he never known that? "You know, I don't think I'm a fan of this feeling."

Garrett just chuckled. "Yeah, not a lot of people are, except for those who are actively in love at the moment. Just keep trying to talk to her, or you're going to have to get used to the idea that she might not be that interested in talking to you. In the meantime, get your head on straight. The only reason Ilsa was even a real problem was because she has been in your life for so long. The kind of woman who you don't really have any feelings for, you don't really care that much about other than surface. You've had a lot of those kinds of women in your life. And on any given Sunday you'd have been all about what Ilsa had to offer. So maybe Sophie wasn't responding to the fact that Ilsa was all over you, but rather responding to all the Ilsas in the world who could come throw a spanner in the works of your relationship." Garrett shrugged. "I don't know. Hey, I'm not a shrink. I'm just your best mate who's trying to get you downstairs for a beer."

"And I appreciate that. But I think there's something I have to do tonight instead."

27

Nathan's stomach twisted and turned. *Shit.* He slammed the door to his flat shut and ran his hands through his hair. He fucked that up. He should have told Ilsa from the get go to stay the fuck away from him.

You should have cut her loose when you started growing feelings. But he hadn't because Ilsa had been convenient. And he hadn't planned on meeting someone like Sophie.

Sophie is supposed to be casual remember? Except it didn't feel casual. It felt like something. And the look on her face when she'd seen him, it felt like something for her too. So ... what? Adam was a rebound guy? *No. Hell no.*

Adam was not the guy she should rebound with. *Rebound guys are fun and flirty, like you.* Fuck had he lost her?

How had he fucked up so spectacularly?

Maybe because you're just like your father? Damn it. This was so fucked.

You're the one who caught a case of feelings. This was supposed to be casual. The problem was, there's nothing casual about Sophie—from her goofy dancing, to that laugh of hers, to the sharp wit and the sharper mind. She wasn't casual. And she was tough. Like the number of times she'd full-on confronted him wearing nothing but a T-shirt and panties, just to tell him he was being an arse-hole. She had no problem doing that. God, he missed that about Sophie. He missed her already. *You are in so much shit right now.* Not only had he broken the rule and become something more than casual, but he'd actually fallen for the girl.

There were days where he just couldn't wait to call her —couldn't wait to tell her everything that was going on with him. She'd been right about that theater company. One purchase to save it had flipped his reality. He was now in talks with a couple of young cinematographers looking for funding. They were looking for financial backing for a movie they couldn't get made. He could help with that. He could effect change in their lives. Then it was something that would honor his mother and make him happy. Sophie had done that. Without her, he would still be spinning his wheels doing the same old thing. There had to be a way to fix this. Shit.

No, there's not. All you can do is what you always do. Block it out, try and forget. Call Garrett and meet him out wherever he was. Drown out the feelings, the pain. Find someone nice and anonymous. Someone who was really casual. *You'll forget her in no time.*

No, he wouldn't forget her. This was going to hurt. Instead of calling his best friend, he made the one call that he'd been avoiding for months.

When she answered, her voice was confused. "Nathan, is everything all right?"

"I hope it's not too late. I know you're a night owl."

His stepmother laughed. "Yes, I am. I was working. I have a new story I'm working on right now." As a thriller writer, she often got wild bouts of inspiration and had to work late into the night. "Are you okay? Shouldn't you be out and about with a date? Or with your mates and things, tearing up the town and giving me a backdrop for one of my books?"

"No, I actually came home early." He wasn't really feeling it, especially not after Sophie had seen him with Ilsa. The look on her face, he would never forget.

"You want to talk about something?"

He wanted to tell her, he did. From the time his father had married her, he felt like he finally had an ally, someone who would at least try to understand him. She'd been exactly what he needed when his father brought her home. And he needed her now just as much as he had then. "Actually, do you mind if I come home?" She paused for just a bit.

"Nathan, this is your home. You never need a reason."

"Okay, in that case, let me hire a car. I'm coming tonight." It was time he faced what he'd been running from.

NATHAN WASN'T sure how he'd managed to sleep in. He arrived home about three in the morning. By that time, Judith had already gone to bed. His father—well, he didn't know exactly where his father was, but it didn't matter to him. Maybe he consciously slept in to avoid the old man. Not like his father would even know he was there. He had taken a car service to come in.

Being at home in his old room was strange. He rarely ever stayed here anymore. Not just because he and his father were estranged either. Once he'd stopped working so closely with his dad, it made sense that he'd want a little more freedom from the constant watchful eyes. The judgment. *Or maybe you didn't want Judith to see that you were just like your old man.*

Maybe that was it.

But not anymore. Everything with Sophie had him all twisted up—even avoiding his own home, the place that he felt most loved and most cared for, all because he couldn't look the woman he loved like his own mother in the eye and he was done with the lies. He wasn't going to be able to deal with his father and move on if he didn't tell her the truth because clearly the old man wasn't going to do it. Throwing on a pair of old joggers, he meandered down the winding staircase to find his stepmother in the sunroom.

"Oh, look who's up. And it's not even noon. I imagine you London types lounging around, not waking yourselves up 'til two. The debauchery of the night before is still clinging to you."

He chuckled. "Somehow I think you picture a wilder evening that I've actually had most of the time."

She scoffed and waved her hand. "I was young once. It's important to enjoy your youth. Before you're so old all you have left is regrets."

He scrubbed a hand through his hair. "Yeah, regrets. So many of them."

Her sharp gaze narrowed. "What's wrong with you? You seem different."

He shook his head. "I'm not different. It's still the same me in trouble more often than not, always misbehaved. See? I haven't changed at all."

Judith shook her head. "No, I remember you being sensitive. Always attuned to what other people were feeling. Maybe that's what's made you so successful with the young ladies. But you genuinely care. In that moment, you make someone feel very special as if they're the only person in your world. That's a great skill to have. People will flock to you. They'll want to be near you."

"Then why do I always feel alone?"

She gave him a soft, sad smile. "That's a matter of perception my darling. But something about you has changed. Perhaps you don't always feel so alone anymore?"

He shrugged. "I don't know. Besides, we're not here to talk about me. I wanted to talk about you."

She went back to her morning tea and took a sip. "Does this have anything to do with the reason you've been avoiding me for the last six months?"

He sighed. "I haven't been avoiding you exactly. I just—I didn't know what to say or do, and so, like a coward, I ran, or rather, didn't say anything. And I feel terrible because you're basically my mother."

"Now you listen to me. You haven't done anything wrong. And I won't have you beating yourself up over it."

He frowned. "Judith, you don't know what I'm going to say."

She laughed. "Don't I? You think I don't know your father well?"

He swallowed hard. "So you knew?"

She shook her head. "Not details, no. But this is not the first time. About nine months ago, he started acting off, distant, and not coming home. Maybe it was my fault. I was buried with some deadline. Not really paying him attention. And then about six months ago, something changed. Then you also stopped coming home. And you are home practically at least once a month. I would call, but you would avoid my calls. Don't act like you weren't avoiding my calls because I know when a call was cut. You would just send me to voicemail and then you would call me back when you had plenty of time to talk."

Nathan leaned forward and clasped his hands together. "I'm such a shit. I'm worse than him in some ways."

She laughed and patted his hand. "No, you're not. You just didn't know when to tell me."

"Well, now I feel even worse because you already knew and I have been avoiding you."

"Well, I didn't know for sure. I knew something was wrong and I had my suspicions. He'd just been distant."

"Why do you put up with him?"

"When you were young, for a long time, I put up with him for you."

"For me?"

"Yes, for you. From the moment I met you, I adored you. You were this little lost boy who just lost his mum. And you needed me. And I had a very good understanding of the kind of man I married. It wasn't exactly what I wanted, but I had the family that I could never have. I have the son that I could never have."

His heart pinched. He'd known that she couldn't have any children. What he hadn't known was she considered him hers as much as he considered her his. "So, you put up with him for me?"

"And for *me*. As soon as I married him and I got you, I had a family. I hadn't really been close to mine. I hadn't had much family to speak of. So even though your dad is a complete twat, he's still my family. And the idea of losing that, the idea of losing you is too much to take."

"You would never lose me."

"Oh yes—now. You're grown. But you guys are still my family—even your father. He'll be back. And honestly, you need not worry. I'm so sorry it has kept you away from me. He'll come back with a tail between his legs and swear to never do it again, and then of course, he'll still do it because that's the core of who he is."

Nathan scrubbed his face with his hands. "So, you're saying that there's absolutely no hope for me. This is who I am. I'm just like him."

Judith shook her head. "No. You are not just like him. You are your own person. Your whole life you think that you're going to turn into him so you sort of fulfilled that prophecy. That's all."

"But I *am* him. I hurt someone and I'm terrified of ever getting close to anyone and of course, the moment that I do, I screw it up."

"The difference between you and your father is when you screw up, you own it. I've never met anyone who takes anything as hard as you do. So, you screw it up, fix it. I've been waiting for this day."

He frowned. "What do you mean 'waiting for this day'?"

"The day you found love, that is."

He frowned. "I'm not in love. I just—I care about her and I hurt her and I don't know how to fix it, and—" He lifted his head when he realized that Judith was laughing. "What the hell is so funny?"

"Sweetheart, you called me yesterday at two in the morning when you should have been out with your mates doing whatever it is that you young lads do. But you called me because you were clearly upset. You asked about this situation with your father, but also about whoever this young woman is. When was the last time you have called me over a girl? And you've had so many."

Shit. She was right. He'd never spoken to Judith about girls. Not because he was embarrassed. It's because none of them really mattered that much. Yeah, sure he'd asked what kind of flowers to get someone. But in terms of actually needing advice, never. "So, what do I do? She saw me with someone and it wasn't what it looked like and hell, I don't know. I mean, we weren't even together. We were casual, and I don't even know how this happened. One moment I'm treating her like everyone else. I'm even trying to help her get dates. The next thing I know, we're watching movies and I'm massaging her feet. And all I want to do is see her smile."

She grinned. "Oh, my boy is finally growing up."

"Yes, yes. I'm growing up. Fair enough, but honestly, what do I do? It hurts. It is so painful."

She nodded. "Yes baby, love often is. So, you messed up. You be straight with her. Direct, make it really clear how you feel, how you messed up and what you plan to do to never do it again. And that's all you can do."

"But what if that's not enough?"

"Well, then you learn for the next time."

"The way I feel? I don't even want to do this again."

"Don't let your father's behavior dictate who you want to be. You are incredible. And your heart has always been so soft. You just walled it off because you've been busy being afraid to be like him. And then because you were so determined to avoid that, you've waited deep, emotional entanglements which actually made you more like him. A whole self-fulfilling prophecy thing. Stop it. Let yourself feel. If you want this girl, go get her. Don't stand by the side and watch her walk away. Fight. Fight for her. That's something your father would never do."

Nathan knew exactly what he needed to do. If he wanted Sophie, he had to show her he was serious. No such thing as casual. Not with her. That's not what he wanted with her. He wanted everything with Sophie. Now he just had to prove it.

28

Four weeks without Nathan.

She missed him. That was the worst part. But the good news was that work kept Sophie busy. Between her night gig which had her out to all hours (she also had her day gig), so that usually meant sleeping for about five hours, waking up and then heading to the nonprofit. No doubt, she preferred the work she did in the daytime. But the work at night kept her going which was fine, because now that she had something that was fulfilling her soul, she didn't mind so much when someone complained about the quality of champagne. She found them amusing.

The one that struck a difference was that she avoided Nathan at all cost. She managed to not see him. Not once in the last two weeks. Maybe he traveled, fucked off to Ibiza or somewhere. Not like it was any of her business or that she cared.

Yes, you do. You miss him. Okay, so fine. She missed him.

No skin off her teeth though, except she missed the sex. God, did she miss the sex.

But she wasn't made to have casual sex. So, while both jobs kept her very busy, she resigned herself to the no boyfriend zone. She just tucked away all the skills that Nathan had taught her because she'd use them some other time when things calmed down.

Uh huh, you mean when you finally get over him?

There was no use arguing with herself. After all, she already knew the truth. She'd gone ahead and fallen in love like a moron. How was she supposed to know that he was secretly really sweet? Except he was also a total player and a womanizer.

No matter how many times she tried to replay that night in her head, all she saw was that woman all over him and him not stopping her. And it hurt. It broke something inside of her every single time. Even when part of her brain tried to offer up explanations: he didn't have his hands on her; he was leaning away from her; she was still sitting on him. And he still hadn't shoved her off of him. So that meant he liked it, right? Or it was easy and available and right there, right? *And you and he were supposed to be casual. Right?*

Yes, okay, so she'd broken the rules. Not that he had exactly. He'd been casual. She'd been the one who broke the rule—the one rule between them, not to get attached.

It was okay though. Who needed a gorgeous sex god in her life? Certainly not her. She was done with men for a while. The gifts started in week three. Not at her doorstep but at her day job. A movie here, popcorn there. Even chocolate chip cookies. Not the hard kind that her mother had always bought but the homemade kind, as if they'd been baked by some master granny from America. At first, she was going to send the gifts back, but she couldn't bring herself to. Besides, who gave back chocolate? He'd even sent her favorite flowers, lilies. No note. Just presents.

The next week, she couldn't help but see him everywhere. She'd gone through this blissful or awful, depending on how you looked about it—time of never seeing him. No matter how much she looked for him she didn't see him anywhere. That's why she had been so convinced he'd moved out. Skulked out in the middle of the night or something.

But now, every morning she left her flat, it didn't matter what time she left, or what time she came home, she would surely run into him. It was as if he had a secret alarm system to tell him every time she opened her door. Every time she was coming up the stairs, he knew. And sure enough, she'd run into him in the hallway. He'd say good morning and she'd ignore him. But it was difficult to ignore him because well, she remembered what he looked like naked. Those blue, stormy eyes always piercing into her. It wasn't cocky or smug like usual; he was polite. If she didn't know better she'd say that he was a perfectly nice, normal neighbor, but he was *everywhere*. When she came home at night, when she woke up in the morning she saw him.

Every single event she had in the evening, sure enough he'd be in attendance. It was not like she didn't know he was supposed to be in attendance. He'd be on the guest list, but somehow, she'd always be surprised when he showed up. He wouldn't stay long. Just long enough so she'd be aware that he'd been there. It was like he was deliberately trying to torture her.

Oh, and the gifts kept coming. Books she'd mentioned she wanted to read; more movies; sometimes cartoons or sketches or cards (never signed), always intended to make her laugh or smile. Just like a billionaire playboy who thought he could buy her affection. But honestly, though, the gifts he was sending, they were personal. They weren't lavish. One was a *Garfield* cartoon strip that he'd cut out of the paper, because she'd mentioned once that she'd fallen in love with *Garfield* after reading the comic in an American newspaper when she was little.

And then, the next week, he brought her coffee in the morning, just how she liked it: black with lots of sugar. She'd open the door in the morning, and he would be there with coffee. She was so surprised the first time she had stumbled back. "Oh my God."

He'd just given her a gentle smile. "I'm not here to bother you. I just brought you coffee." As you did. As if he'd been doing that every day for their entire relationship, or not relationship. Whatever.

And it happened again the next day, and the next. It had been like that for another week. In addition to gifts turning up where she worked, it was like he was slowly applying pressure. How in the world was she supposed to stay mad at him *and* avoid him? It was extremely difficult. Even she wasn't that stubborn.

The following week, she was determined to avoid him. But he wasn't there for coffee. Thank God.

Even Gemma had started to laugh. "You say you don't

want him and that you're annoyed, but now you're mad when he doesn't show up for coffee?"

"But it's like he's tempting me. Showing me what it could be like. And then he vanishes."

Her best friend found it endlessly entertaining. Gemma didn't understand. She thought it was sweet.

That evening, he was waiting for her after work. "Listen," she said, "I am exhausted and I don't know what kind of mind fuck you have going on, but I can't fight with you right now."

Instead of a smug smirk, he looked genuinely concerned. "You've been working a lot."

She sighed. "Yes, I have. I still have my regular job, and I took on some nonprofit work."

He frowned. "Are they paying you?"

She shook her head. "I took it because I *wanted* to. It was just like I always talked about."

Then the grin broke out. "Oh, Sophie, I'm chuffed. That's amazing. It's exactly what you wanted. You'll be brilliant."

She nodded. "Yes, brilliant, but first I need sleep, so if you don't have a reason you're leaning against my doorway, I'd rather get to bed please."

"Actually, yes, there is a reason I'm leaning against your doorway. I'd like to ask you to dinner."

She frowned. "Why?"

"Well, for starters, I figured we should talk."

She shook her head. "There's not much to talk about. We had an arrangement. I clearly broke it and got emotionally attached. Now you don't want to see me anymore. Except, I don't know what you're doing with the gifts and the things and all of that."

He cleared his throat. "I don't want it to be over."

"But you said casual. I clearly wanted to take it further and then that woman—"

He shook his head. "Come to dinner with me. I'll explain."

"You know I can't—I just—I'm tired. I need to sleep."

He nodded. "Fair enough."

The next morning, she didn't see him. Again, there was no coffee. He was such a tease.

Luckily, she didn't have to work an event that night, so she went to her one job and went home. But, there he was again. "Oh my God. What now?"

He just smiled. "I'm here to ask you out to dinner."

"I swear to God, you are the most infuriating human being I have ever met. We don't have anything left to say to each other."

He nodded. "Okay. I'll see you tomorrow, Soph."

Exasperation tumbled out of her in a laugh. "Oh my God, why are you doing this? It's like you're torturing me, or trying to drive me completely mad."

"Neither of those. I just know that you don't believe this. You don't think we could be great. And so, I need to show you. I need to prove it to you, so that's what I'm doing until you realize that I'm serious."

"Serious about what? We had a casual thing. I blew it out of proportion."

He leaned in close to her and she held her breath. Oh

God, he smelled so good. Immediately her body softened and ripened. Her nipples grew tight.

Traitors.

Her core contracted and she tried not to inhale any further, because God, it might be entirely possible to orgasm from his smell alone. "What are you trying to say?"

"I'm trying to tell you that it was more than casual for me too. That last time it was different. I could feel myself falling. I knew what was happening. But I know I can't just tell you. I need to show you. So, have a good night. I'll see you tomorrow."

Sophie threw up her arms. "Oh my God, if I go to dinner with you, will you stop?"

He shook his head. "No. If you go to dinner with me, you won't want me to stop."

29

Sophie's feet hurt. As a matter of fact, everything hurt. But God, she felt good. And she was going to reward herself with a cookie. Today's hard work had paid off. She'd been right. Charity fund raising stuff was far more rewarding. It didn't necessarily pay the bills, but even if she was exhausted at the end of the day, she felt amazing.

She was enjoying the rare springtime, London sunshine when she popped into the bakery around the corner from her flat. James, the bloke who worked behind the counter at the bakery smiled at her when he saw her. "Oh, you've got a smile on your face. Good news?"

Sophie grinned. "Yeah, it was a good day. I will take three of the ginger biscuits and two of the American style chocolate chip cookies please."

"Coming right up."

She tried not to fiddle with the hem of her jumper as she waited. Just as he handed her the bag of goodies, and she paid him with her stripe card, something caught her eye. She looked up and frowned as she looked down the street.

No. It can't be. Your mind is just playing tricks on you. It's not him.

Lately, *him*, had been Nathan. Every waking thought had been consumed with him. But after a couple of weeks the pain wasn't as acute now. More of a dull throbbing. Luckily, with work, she could think about something else. She could focus on something else. And now this? She couldn't take one more life disruption right now.

It's not him, relax.

She threw a few coins into the tip jar for James and then dashed out of the bakery. The throng of people only increased the closer she got to Piccadilly Circus, but finally, the man up ahead of her made a right and she caught up to him. The closer she got, her skin hummed and she knew she was right. It's him. "Dad?"

The man with his tall frame and dark hair inclined his head as he turned. His eyes went wide when he recognized her. "Sophie, sweetheart. Imagine running into you on the street."

She frowned. "Yeah, well, it happens." Just not with him.

He lumbered over to her and awkwardly bent to give her a hug. "You look well, darling. All right then? You know, I was going to call you. I just have been busy. I just got to town and –"

She'd long gotten used to his excuses. The reasons he wasn't around and why he couldn't be bothered to call her, or send her a birthday card, or any of those things. But seeing him in her city in the flesh as if it was perfectly normal, that was just taking the piss. "Dad, what are you doing here?"

"Well, I'm just meeting a mate 'round the corner."

She blinked up at him. "A mate? Like, you're just popping 'round for tea with a mate? Dad, you lived in Dover. You can't even call your only daughter when you come to town?"

"Oh Soph, don't be like that. I honestly wasn't thinking about it. It was a last minute thing."

A blonde woman came around the corner and smiled as she approached them. "Richard, there you are. You're late as usual. Did you forget what time we were meeting?" She turned her gaze to Sophie and then eyed her up and down, as if assessing her at fret level. "And who do we have here?"

Sophie shot her father a glance. "Hi, I'm Sophie. I'm the daughter."

The woman stared at him for a moment. "Richard, this is your daughter? You said she traveled and wouldn't be available."

Her father shifted uncomfortably. "Shit, the thing is, Michelle, Sophie haven't seen each other for a while, so I didn't want to spring a new relationship on her. And Sophie, of course, I was going to call you and introduce you to my —"

Sophie shook her head and put her hand out. "Girlfriend."

Michelle, her father's new girlfriend could easily have been her older sister. That was beside the point. The point was, her own father hadn't reached out when he was in her city. "Like I said, it's nice to see you. Nice to meet you. I have to go dad. I've had a long day," she said, feeling suddenly deflated.

"Oh come on Soph, don't be like that. I'm sorry. It's just, I wanted a little alone time with Michelle before I gave you a call."

Yeah, that didn't seem to go well with Michelle either. "Dad, I'm your daughter. You can't even call me? You know what, forget it. It's fine. Michelle, you seem very nice. You seem lovely. Dad, I wish I could say I'm surprised, but I'm not. The truth is, you've never been that father who would call and tell me, 'Hey, love, I'm here in your city. Let's have coffee, or tea, or hell, let me stay with you.' I know who you are. To be fair, yeah, I'm not sure why I'm surprised."

His brow furrowed. "That doesn't mean I don't love you."

Sophie set her lips into a firm line. "All I know is that you're my Dad. It would have been nice to know you were here." Sophie nodded a goodbye to Michelle and turned away from her father heading back toward her flat.

"Soph, Sophie, wait."

She whipped back around. "What? What do you have to say? There's nothing left to say. This is you. The bloke who's never around, whether I need you or not, you're just not really present. In and out with pretty young things, I see you're still doing that."

"So I like to be sociable and date. And I'm very busy for work."

"Yes, you're a very talented musician. I'm glad you get

to play all over the place, but you know what, growing up, it would have been nice to have my Dad be there for me. And as an adult, it would have been nice to know my father was in town. But right now, I'm tired and I need to go back to my flat."

"Look, maybe we can have –"

She shook her head. "No, because I'll just be so disappointed when you don't turn up. And honestly, after years of these kinds of disappointments, I can't take it. I love you, Dad. Have fun with Michelle. She seems nice."

"Sophie, you know I love you. I'm just not good at the responsibility part. Having a kid was a lot for me. Your kids count on you. Everyone counts on you. I'm not really good at it. And I know I let you down a lot."

"Let me down? That's an understatement. Do you realize that I can't even have a normal relationship because of you? I'm just not capable of it. I date all these guys that look right on paper, like they would be great fathers, or providers, or that sort of thing. And I avoid dating them like you. The thing is, the man I fell in love with is exactly someone like you. Not emotionally available, not really around, popular with the women. God, was doomed to repeat history."

He frowned. "Sophie, love, listen. My mistakes, my problems, they're not yours. I messed up as a father. I messed up now. I wanted to call you. I knew the right thing to do. I knew the thing that I wanted to do, but I made the excuses because I know it would be hard. That this conversation would be hard. So, I avoided it. But that's me. You said you've fallen in love with a bloke. Is he nice?"

She shrugged. "It turns out he's not *that* nice, a little too much like my Dad."

He winced and she immediately regretted her words. "I suppose I deserved that." He shifted on his feet. "Listen, I know I'm doing this the wrong way, but tonight Michelle has to work, and I've got another two nights before I head back to Dover. I would like to see my daughter if she would let me. Please."

She considered this for a moment, letting his words sink in. "Yeah, I'd like to Dad, but honestly, I'm not entirely sure you'd show."

"Yeah, you're right. The old me wouldn't, but I want you to know that people are capable of change. Michelle and I, we've been doing this thing back and forth, and I like her. And I've been putting in the effort. I think you two would get along. I'd like to start getting on the right road with you. I'd really like it."

She nodded resolutely. "I'd like that too. Okay, tomorrow night then?"

He grinned. "Good. I'll ring your mobile. And Soph?"

She paused before turning, "Yeah, Dad."

"The young man – the one that's maybe too much like me, does he love you back?"

She shrugged. "I don't know. I thought he did."

"He messed up then?"

"You know, I don't really even know. I thought I saw something… I don't know. The point is, I got too attached."

"You know what, Sophie darling? Sometimes attachment is good. It can make sure that you come back to where you're supposed to be all along."

As she watched her father… the man who had been in and out of her life, more out than in, he did seem different. Calmer, somehow… maybe Michelle was responsible for it. Either way, she had a date with her father for the first time in nearly a decade.

As it turned out, Nathan might have been right about dinner. In the end, she agreed because she knew that she would just keep finding him on her doorstep until she finally said yes. But, also, a tiny part of her missed him. As always, Nathan was charming and fun. He talked to her about the work that he'd started doing. The projects he was investing in. And he asked her endless questions about her job—so many that she was even tired of answering them. Finally, they got around to the part of the conversation that she'd been dreading most of the night.

"Come on, let's have it. Your explanation so we don't have to keep doing the runaround in circles then."

"The woman, Ilsa, she was another casual arrangement I had. Before you. Not even an arrangement. Just a date to some charity things." He swallowed. "And we slept together sometimes. Nothing regular and nothing we even talked about. I was clear about what we were and what we weren't."

Sophie frowned. "But you said that you weren't casual with anyone else at the time when you were sleeping with me."

He shook his head. "And I wasn't. From the moment

you and I started, I stopped calling her. She was a bit upset when I saw her at the club. She wanted to know why I hadn't taken her to some event. I guess, apparently, she wanted more than casual too."

"There seems to be a lot of that going around."

"I guess there was. I swear to Christ, I didn't touch her." He shook his head. "I should've pushed her away sooner. I had no idea how to navigate any of this. But I was moving away from her and she sat on me and I didn't move quickly enough. I know. There are some habits I have that I need to break, but you have to know I would never hurt you, not on purpose. That's not the kind of person I am. I don't *want* to be him. I don't want to be my father."

She winced. "I never said you were. I just—It hurt seeing you with her. I knew I wasn't supposed to develop feelings, but that was awful."

He bit his lip. "It—hurt seeing you with that prat. And that smug git—I swear to God, I wanted to hit him."

"I appreciate your restraint. I needed to try and go out with someone."

Nathan cursed under his breath. "Why?"

"For starters, my life. I was really lonely. Just like you've tried to avoid being your father, I've tried to avoid ending up with someone like mine. I never stopped to think about who I might actually want long term. I made practical decisions and then with you it was like I made the most impractical decision in the world. On paper you were all wrong. And you made it clear you didn't want me long term. But you were the one I wanted. I needed to move past it the best I could. I was convinced I was doomed to want things that weren't good for me."

Nathan frowned and she could see the pain etched on his face. "I know I fucked up but I am good for you. You're the only one I want to tell everything too and when I'm with you, fuck, I don't know, I feel lighter. Like I'm not carrying all this shit around all the time. I can be that for you too. Give me a chance to show you."

She heard the sincerity in the deep timber of his voice. She could practically feel the tangible truth. But she wasn't willing to pretend with him anymore. "I'm not going back to just us shagging. I'm not good at that sort of ambiguous relationship."

"That's good. Because somewhere along the line, between movie Saturdays and your attempts at a Sunday roast I fell in love with you. I certainly don't want to go back to that. Hell, I never really wanted that either. It sucked to see you with him. To see you with anyone other than me. To think of his hands on you." He shook his head. "You belong with me. I just didn't know it when we started. I thought this feeling in my chest, the warmth, was an anomaly."

She started at him, her heart caught in her throat. Had he just said he loved her? Had she actually heard those words? "You never had to worry about anything. He wasn't the one I wanted. It was you. Even when I didn't know it was you, it was you."

He frowned and asked softly, "You didn't sleep with him?"

Sophie threw up her hands. "How many times do I have

to tell you? I'm not good at casual. And I have this thing for my neighbor who honestly, can be a bit of a thick prick at times."

He chuckled. "Oh yeah?"

She realized what she'd said then groaned even as she laughed. "Oh my God. You're incorrigible. You know what I mean. I took your stupid lessons just to be near you."

"So, we're clear, you never did need any lessons from me. You blew my mind without even trying."

A flush crept up her neck. "Thank you. I am brilliant. So, what happens now?"

He swallowed. "Well, now I show you that I plan on loving you until you make me go … "

"How are you going to do that?"

He smiled. "Come with me. I want to show you something."

~

"Oh, Nathan! This theater—you saved it."

He nodded. "I did. We started to do some renovations and started up rehearsals again. They'll be putting on *Rent* in a matter of months."

"I'm really proud of you. I'm sure your mother would have been too."

Nathan intertwined his hand with hers and then tugged her up the stairs. "C'mon, we can watch some of the rehearsals from up here."

While the DJ thumped a heavy hip-hop-infused pop beat, and the actors on stage danced and sang, he ran his fingertips just under Sophie's skirt. She paid him no attention, just continued moving to the beat.

He brushed her thick hair off the nape of her neck and kissed her softly. "I want to touch you."

She turned in his arms. "I want to be touched. I've missed you, Nathan."

Missing her wasn't even the right word for him. He *craved* her. They'd only been apart a little over a month, but he felt like a part of him had been cut out.

Nathan slid his fingers up her thigh until he reached the silken heat between. "Jesus, Sophie. It's been too long."

When he slid a finger inside her, she reached behind her and grabbed the ledge. Down below, Mimi belted "Out Tonight." The rest of the cast joined her dancing on stage. All the while, he slowly penetrated Sophie, teasing her slick opening with his questing fingers. Tormenting himself.

She reached for him and tugged on his belt. Knowing what she wanted, what she needed, what they both craved, Nathan made quick work of his pants. When he reached for his wallet, she shook her head. "I—I got on the pill. I, um, did it before ... "

"Fuck, Sophie." He dropped his forehead to hers. "Are you sure?"

She nodded. "I love you." She blurted out. "I should have probably told you earlier at dinner. I just, couldn't believe you were saying the words to me."

Nathan swallowed. "You saying them or not. I know it. I can see it in the way you look at me. I can feel it when you smile at me. The words are just a bonus."

She blinked up at him rapidly. "Look who's a romantic."

He couldn't help the smirk. "A dirty romantic. Do you want me to fuck you bare?" he asked through clenched teeth.

She tensed for a moment, then shivered as he stroked her slit again. "Yes," she whispered. "Please." Before she'd even finished speaking, she'd taken his cock in her closed fist and was stroking it up and down rhythmically.

With every stroke and dip of his tongue, she rocked back against him. Sophie moaned against his lips as she tilted her body into his. He'd thought his cock was hard earlier, but damn, there was hard, then there was whatever the hell was happening to him. Like the sexual tension had turned his dick into pure steel. *Take your time, wanker. Do not blow this. For her or for you.*

Shit, he wanted more, needed more. He could kiss her all day. She was tentative at first, but with every stoke of his tongue, she softened, opening for him, baring a little bit of her heart. Jesus, what was she doing to him? His skin tingled like someone was lighting it on fire from the inside. It made him hot. Tight. Itchy. And the only cure was to keep touching this woman.

Who the hell was he kidding? Even if she said to stop right now, he'd still beg to be near her. He'd keep his feelings to himself because he just wanted to be near her. *Holy shit.* If he didn't do something, he'd lose hold of the cords of his control. He wanted her. And he had a feeling a lifetime wouldn't be enough.

He was so focused on watching as she arched her back, offering up her breasts to him, that he barely heard her. "Mmm?" Shifting slightly, he kissed her again as he tested the weight of her breasts and teased the pebbled tips with his thumbs. "Is this what you needed?" he whispered against her lips.

Sophie dug her nails into his hair, attempting to pull him closer still. Fuck, she was hot. So hot. She moaned into his mouth as he teased her other nipple. He swallowed the mewling sounds that slid from her lips.

The music below was so loud no one would hear them. But the thrill and possibility of getting caught kept the buzz humming over his skin.

"No. Don't stop."

A smile tugged at his lips. "But I have other plans." Trailing kisses along her stomach, he stopped at her belly button to dip his tongue inside, tasting her.

He kissed lower still. "Open your legs for me, Sophie."

She lifted her head and met his gaze. "Nathan, what are you—?"

"You can be patient, can't you?" Shit, like he could. There was still a distinct chance he might come in his boxers. But fuck, he really hoped not. "A little wider. Yeah, that's it. Like that. I like to see what I'm doing."

Her muscles tensed. "Nathan, oh my God!"

"Do you trust me?"

She swallowed but then nodded.

A smile tugged at his lips. "Okay, that's good. I plan on doing a few dirty things to you. Helps if you trust me."

She snorted a laugh and then tried to close her legs, but he kept them firmly apart. "Okay, okay."

He kissed her inner thighs again, relishing in the strength in them. She was so wet already. He loved it.

Tracing his knuckles across her slick folds, he teased apart the lips of her sex. "You are so pretty, Sophie. Soft and delicate. I think I need a taste. What do you say, Sophie? Do you want my tongue on your clit?"

Her reply was a whispered, "Y-yes."

"Okay, good." Kissing her softly, just above her mound, he used his thumbs to separate the slick flesh, and she whimpered. Leaning forward, he lapped at her folds with his tongue. Her hips bucked off the seat, and he stopped immediately. "You okay? I'm just getting started. Maybe you should hold on to something."

"W—wow. Oh my… God. Yeah. I'm okay."

He grinned. "You like that, then?"

She grinned down at him. "Uh, I don't know. You'd better try again, so we can be sure."

"Coming right up. In the name of science, of course."

She giggled again but stopped when he applied firm, lazy licks from her cleft to her clitoris. She didn't say much after that. Just moaning and some shaking. He dipped his tongue into her core, working it in as far as it would go, lapping up her juices as he gently made love to her with his tongue.

It didn't take long before her thighs began to quake. Even with his tongue, he could feel the tiny tremors. Feeling the inner walls of her sex as they contracted around his tongue.

When she threw her head back, muttering something incomprehensible, he gently brushed his thumb over her tight pucker. Her resounding scream and freefall from orgasm had him smiling even as he gently continued to suck her clit.

While she came, he kept up the steady rhythm. Stoking the flames until she came down then crashed again.

"Nathan, I can't. Please—"

He kissed his way back up her body. Pausing at her nipples again, he gently scraped one with his teeth. When she gasped, he wrapped his lips around her nipple. Languidly, she slid her arms around his neck.

He wanted to see if he could get just one more orgasm from her. Just one. Then he'd stop being greedy.

His teeth scraped her nipple again as he eased a finger into her. The telltale flutter of her core around his finger had him cursing low as her tight, slick channel clutched at him.

"You are so unbelievably beautiful," he muttered against her flesh. "Let me feel how much you want me." He withdrew the one and slid in two.

Sophie whimpered, and Nathan squeezed his eyes shut. He needed to come. But he could wait for her. Just one more. That was all he wanted. Hooking his fingers inside her, he teased her G-spot. He wanted to take his time with her now because once he had his dick inside her, there'd be no exploration, no taking his time. He was too raw. Too ready. He'd been riding the edge of need since he met her.

Since he'd almost lost her.

Nathan shook his head again. "I should have told you from the get go, Sophie. You were never casual for me. And now that you're mine, I'm never letting you go."

Sophie held on to the railing and shifted her stance to make room for him between her thighs.

Nathan grazed his teeth against her neck. "What are you doing to me?"

"No more than you're doing to me," she whispered.

As he sank into her, inch by inch, her big eyes widened, and she moaned low. He retreated until only the tip of his cock was still inside her, then he sank in again. *That's it, nice and steady. You can do this. Not too fast. You'll be—fine. Holy fuck.* Her inner walls milked him, and his eyes crossed as the tingling fire burst forth from the base of his spine.

And while Mimi sang below, Nathan sank deep.

He was going to come. And from the fire racing over his skin, he was going to be out, but not before making her break apart again. But when he slid his hand over her taut belly and stroked his finger over her clit, she started to shake. *Jackpot.*

Again and again, he stroked her clit, adjusting their position so that she stood straight, holding on to the railing. From the stage, if anyone looked up, they might only see her shoulders. They wouldn't see what he was doing to her. No one would see how completely she owned him.

Or that he was on his knees and her legs splayed were played wide. Holding her legs wider, he circled her clit with his thumb and his cock sank deep.

Would it always be like this with her? Would he keep wanting her this badly as if he'd never had her? With each slide home and retreat, when the harsh cry tore out of her throat, her body convulsed around his cock like a vise, and Nathan lost any thread of control he might have once had. He marked her as his forever.

EPILOGUE

Nathan fingered the lock of Sophie's red hair. "You know I've always liked the red."

She cuddled into him and kissed his pectoral muscle. "It feels good to have it back."

"Don't ever change it. It reminds me of that first night I met you. The way you were watching me." He winked.

She giggled even as she took a bite. "*You* were watching me. And you were being very naughty. I'll remind you."

She was right. He had been naughty, but she liked it. "You like it, don't you?"

He snuggled into the crook of her neck and kissed her and a shiver ran into her body. "You have to tell me if you don't like it, then I won't ever do it again."

She giggled. "Well, let's not be too hasty. I mean, you were naughty, but you were sexy, so, you know, that sort of canceled out."

Nathan kissed at her neck and Sophie arched her back automatically as he moved closer to her nipples. *Shit.* He could not get distracted right now. He had important things to ask her. Things he was terrified she would say no too. But he needed to ask her because he wanted them to be together. Lazily, he brushed his lips over one nipple and she moaned, running her fingers through his hair, drawing him closer.

"Easy sweetheart, I'll get there. But first, I want to ask you something."

Why was he so nervous? This was Sophie. Everything with her was so easy. He could just be himself. And working together had only brought them closer. She'd taken the theater on as one of her clients. Thanks to her, opening week was completely sold out.

So, why are you scared?

Because there was still the chance that she could say no... that she didn't want this with him.

"Nathan, come on. Please –"

"I promise. But first, I wanted to ask you how you felt about taking our two apartments and making them one. As a matter of fact, how would you feel if we bought the two of them and the upstairs garden?"

He stilled. Waiting, holding his breath, trying to tell his heart to calm down.

Sophie though, she was no fool. She knew what he was really asking. "So, you're asking me to move in with you?"

"Yeah. I am." He was asking for a whole lot more than that. But he figured he'd go with baby steps. "What do you say?"

He lifted his head to meet her gaze to find her smile was brilliant. "Well, considering I spend the majority of my time here, or running backward and forward naked in the hallway between here and there, I suppose we could do something like that. But Nathan, I can't afford to buy either of these places. And I don't want you paying my way."

He knew what she was getting at. It pinched a little still, even though he understood why. He'd met Sophie's Dad. She said he was different now, but he could see she was still wary of him. It made him worry that she was waiting for him to leave. Well he would just have to show her that he was never leaving. For him, she was his world. He was all in.

"I know you feel weird. At first, I was thinking you just chip in what you can pay. But I actually have a better idea. It's something I've been thinking about for a while."

She frowned. "Yeah?"

"Yeah. It's probably something I've been thinking about since the first night on the balcony at the theater."

She giggled. "Oh, I remember that. But you'll have to enlighten me. Exactly what part were you thinking about?"

"Well, I was thinking about how before that I've been terrified that I'd fallen in love with you and you didn't love me back."

She ran her hand gently through his hair. "Of course, I love you. I didn't want to, but I did."

He nodded. "When you finally said it, I thought my heart was going to burst. I was so happy. And all I could think about was how I wanted you in my arms with me *forever.*"

Her smile was soft, although her brows slightly furrowed as if she sensed where the conversation was going. "I wanted to ask you then, but it was too soon. So, I've been thinking about doing this every day since then, how I would do it. All the lavish, ridiculous ways I could possibly ask you."

Now she sat up, her eyes going wide. Nathan kissed his way up her chest and onto her collarbone, into the crook of her neck, finally along her jaw and then her lips. "And I fully plan to do one of those ridiculous, lavish things. But for the first time I asked you, I wanted it to be just you and me, Nathan and Sophie."

He reached over to the bedside table, and pulled out the small velvet box. And then maneuvered himself so that he was on one knee on the bed. "Sophie, I don't even know my life began really when I met you. The year after that, you haunted my dreams. I couldn't quite get you out of them. And then when I realized you were my neighbor, you dug in and took hold. I've never loved anyone more than I love you in this moment and every moment. Will you do me the honor of being my wife?"

Sophie clasped her hands over her mouth. And then her eyes welled with tears. When she dropped her hands, she stared at him. "Nathan! Oh my God! Oh my God!"

His lips tipped into a smirk. "You still haven't said the right word, sweetheart. You're making me rather nervous." And then he realized he hadn't actually opened the box to show her the ring.

Would she like it? When he started to open it, he said, "Well maybe I should show you this first."

She grabbed the box from him and slammed it shut. "I don't want to see it. It could be a piece of cardboard for all I care, I just want you. The best moments I've had in the last year and a half had been just like this, in your arms. Talking, and watching movies, and eating popcorn, and hanging out. I don't want anything else. Just you."

Nathan wrapped an arm around her and pulled her up against him. "Is that so? So, you're telling me you don't want this ring that I painstakingly picked just for you?"

She laughed. "Well, I don't *need* it. But since you went through all that effort, maybe I should just see it."

Nathan laughed. "Happy to oblige." When he lifted the velvet box she gasped. "Oh Nathan, it's perfect."

He could have gone gaudy and ostentatious. After all, that was sort of his style. But for Sophie, he wanted a very simple statement. And so, the band was ultra-thin with very tiny diamonds circling it, with a brilliant cut solitaire sat on top. He showed remarkable restraint giving her a ring that was only two karats. Because there had been this five karat one that he wanted but he figured Sophie would be ticked off with him if he got her that one. At least this one she could wear in public. It didn't matter though. She was right. As long as they were together everything was perfect. "So, will you marry me then?"

She nodded. "You better believe I will."

Nathan pulled the ring from the confines of the box and then delicately placed it on her finger. It was a perfect fit. Just like the two of them.

THANK YOU

Thank you for reading MR DIRTY! I hope you enjoyed my London Billionaire.

Would you like to know when my next book is available? You can sign up for my new release newsletter here.

Visit me at www.nanamalone.com, follow me on twitter at @NanaMalone, or like my Facebook page at www.facebook.com/nanamalonewriter. And if you want to chat with other peeps who love my books and spread the word, you can join my Sassy Street Team here!

Reviews help other readers find books. I appreciate all reviews. Please leave a review on your retailer's site or on Goodreads to help other readers discover the Protectors Series.

Don't miss any of the London Billionaire Standalones

Mr. Trouble

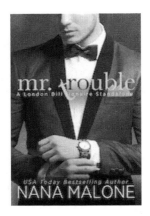

Mr. Big

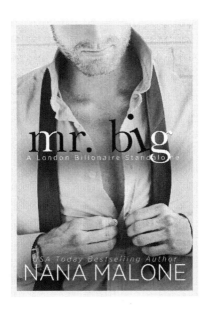

Mr. Dirty

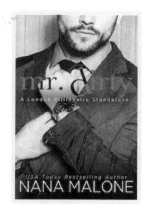

NANA MALONE READING LIST

Looking for a few Good Books? Look no Further

London Billionaires Standalones
Mr. Trouble (Jarred & Kinsley)
Mr. Big (Zach & Emma)
Mr. Dirty(Nathan & Sophie)

The Shameless World

Shameless
Shame
Shameless
Shameful
Unashamed
Shameless Bonus

The Force Duet
Forceful

Force

Enforce

The Deep Duet
***Deep - Coming 2018

***Deeper - Coming 2018

The Player
Bryce

Dax

Echo

Fox

Ransom

Gage

The Donovans Series
Come Home Again (Nate & Delilah)

Love Reality (Ryan & Mia)

Race For Love (Derek & Kisima)

Love in Plain Sight (Dylan and Serafina)

Eye of the Beholder – (Logan & Jezzie)

***Love Struck (Zephyr & Malia) - Expected 2018

The In Stilettos Series
Sexy in Stilettos (Alec & Jaya)

Sultry in Stilettos (Beckett & Ricca)

Sassy in Stilettos (Caleb & Micha)

Strollers & Stilettos (Alec & Jaya & Alexa)

Seductive in Stilettos (Shane & Tristia)

Stunning in Stilettos (Bryan & Kyra)

**Sinful in Stilettos - Expected 2018*

~~~

In Stilettos Spin off

Tempting in Stilettos (Serena & Tyson)
Teasing in Stilettos (Cara & Tate)
Tantalizing in Stilettos (Jaggar & Griffin)

The Chase Brothers Series

London Bound (Alexi & Abbie)
London Calling (Xander & Imani)

Love Match Series (Contemporary Romance)

*Game Set Match (Jason & Izzy)
Mismatch (Eli & Jessica)

Temptation Series

Corporate Affairs
Exposed
The Flirtation

The Protectors Series (Superhero Romance)

*Betrayed a Reluctant Protector Prequel
Reluctant Protector (Cassie & Seth)
Forsaken Protector (Symone & Garrett)
Wounded Protector (Jansen & Lisa)

The Hit & Run Bride Contemporary Romance Series

Hit & Run Bride (Liam & Becca)

Hit & Miss Groom (Alex & Vanessa)
Hit the Billionaire Jackpot (Jenna & Jacob)

Harlequin Kimani Books
Wrapped in Red (Linc and Nomi)
Tonight (Tristan and Synthia)
Vow of Seduction (Elina & Gabe)
Unwrapping the Holidays (Jamie & Cole)
This is Love (Bennett & Val)
Never Christmas Without You (Justin & Alex)

Don't want to miss a single release? Click here!

*Free Read
**Upcoming release. Dates Subject to Change

ABOUT NANA MALONE

USA Today Bestselling Author, Nana Malone's love of all things romance and adventure started with a tattered romantic suspense she borrowed from her cousin on a sultry summer afternoon in Ghana at a precocious thirteen. She's been in love with kick butt heroines ever since. Nana is the author of multiple series. And the books in her series have been on multiple Amazon Kindle and Barnes & Noble bestseller lists as well as the iTunes Breakout Books list and most notably the USA Today Bestseller list.

Want to get notified of Nana's next book? Text SASSY to 313131!

About Nana Malone

Made in the USA
Columbia, SC
20 December 2017